The Mystery
of the Missing Tiger
and Other Stories

Laura E. Williams

SCHOLASTIC INC.

New York Toronto London Auckland Sydney
Mexico City New Delhi Hong Kong Buenos Aires

The Mystery of the Dark Lighthouse, ISBN-13: 978-0-439-21726-2, ISBN-10: 0-439-21726-1. Copyright © 2000 by Roundtable Press, Inc., and Laura E. Williams.

The Mystery of Dead Man's Curve, ISBN-13: 978-0-439-21725-5, ISBN-10: 0-439-21725-3. Copyright © 2000 by Roundtable Press, Inc., and Laura E. Williams.

The Mystery of the Missing Tiger, ISBN-13: 978-0-439-21728-6, ISBN-10: 0-439-21728-8. Copyright © 2001 by Roundtable Press, Inc., and Laura E. Williams.

12 11 10 9 8 7 6 5 4 3 2 1   7 8 9 10 11/0

Printed in the U.S.A.   23

This edition created exclusively for Barnes & Noble, Inc.

2007 Barnes & Noble Books

ISBN-13: 978-0-7607-9653-5
ISBN-10: 0-7607-9653-X

First compilation printing, June 2007

A Roundtable Press Book

Contents

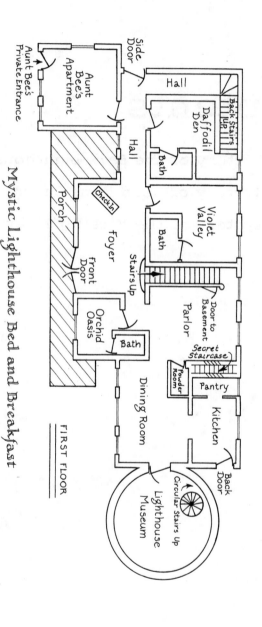

Mystic Lighthouse Bed and Breakfast

FIRST FLOOR

Side Door

Hall

Back Stairs Up

Daffodil Den

Bath

Aunt Bee's Apartment

Aunt Bee's Private Entrance

Hall

Check In

Porch

Foyer

Violet Valley

Bath

Stairs Up

Front Door

Door to Basement

Orchid Oasis

Parlor

Bath

Secret Staircase

Powder Room

Pantry

Dining Room

Kitchen

Back Door

Lighthouse Museum

Circular Stairs Up

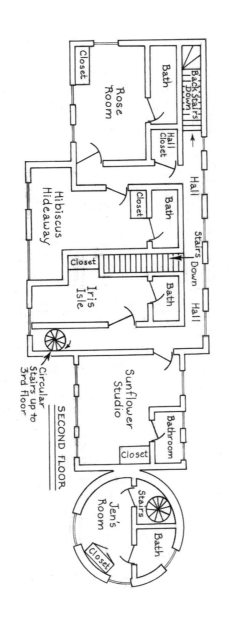

Closet

Bath

Rose
Room

Back Stairs
Down

Hall
Closet

Hall

Closet

Bath

Hibiscus
Hideaway

Stairs Down

Closet

Iris
Isle

Bath

Hall

Circular
Stairs Up to
3rd Floor

Sunflower
Studio

SECOND FLOOR

Bathroom

Closet

Stairs

Jen's
Room

Bath

Closet

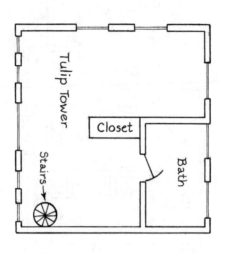

Tulip Tower

Closet

Bath

Stairs→

THIRD FLOOR

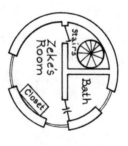

Zeke's Room

Stairs

Bath

Closet

Note to Reader

Welcome to *The Mystery of the Missing Tiger and Other Stories*, where YOU solve the mystery. As you read, look for clues pointing to the guilty person. There are blank suspect sheets in the back of this book. You can copy them to keep track of the clues you find throughout all three stories. They are the same as the suspect sheets that Jen and Zeke will use later in each story when they try to solve the mysteries. Can you solve the mysteries before they can?

Good luck!

The Mystery
of the Dark
Lighthouse

This book is for Marilyn Cozad,
a fellow mystery buff

Contents

1

Ghost!

Completely out of breath, Jen flung open the front door of the Mystic Lighthouse Bed and Breakfast and raced inside. Her twin brother, Zeke, followed closely behind her. Aunt Bee handed each of them a towel. The twins had lived with their aunt in the B&B since their parents' death when they were only two years old. Uncle Cliff, Aunt Bee's husband, had died a couple of years ago, so Aunt Bee was all the family they had left.

"I hate this rain," Jen complained. Even with a raincoat on, she'd gotten soaked.

Zeke hung his dripping green slicker on the coat-rack, next to Jen's. He rubbed his hair with the warm, dry towel. "The Mystic bicentennial cookout will be canceled tomorrow."

"I'm afraid you're right," Aunt Bee agreed. "This is just the edge of the storm—it's supposed to pour all weekend. We may even get some hail."

With a towel draped across her damp shoulders, Jen stared outside into the stormy darkness. The trees twisted in the wind, and lightning flashed over the churning ocean. "I hope we don't lose power again."

"We always lose electricity being this far out," Zeke said glumly. "Not only will the storm keep me from sailing, I won't be able to play computer games, either."

Aunt Bee grinned. "But think of all the chores you'll get done!"

The twins worked hard to help their aunt keep the B&B running smoothly. Cleaning rooms was easy, and the guests were usually interesting to meet and talk to. Jen and Zeke also helped at mealtimes, especially if Aunt Bee was serving more than the usual breakfast that she offered the guests every day. Under special circumstances, Aunt Bee also prepared lunch and dinner for them.

Once they were somewhat dried off, the twins followed their aunt across the foyer to the check-in counter. There she had already laid out several flashlights, extra batteries, three oil lamps, and a number of candles. Flashlights were fine, Aunt Bee always said, but lamps and candles created a cozy old-time feel.

"Get into dry clothes, then come back and help me get these ready," Aunt Bee instructed, trimming one of the lamp wicks.

Zeke glanced at the registration book. "Have some people already checked in?" he asked.

"Lenore and Karen Mills are in the Sunflower Studio," Aunt Bee replied. "Driving from the airport in this weather wore them out and they're resting."

"Dead Man's Curve is bad enough on a sunny day," Zeke said, picturing the hairpin turns on the road to the B&B, with the cliff dropping off abruptly to the rocks and foaming ocean far below. Somehow the short guardrail along the edge didn't seem like enough protection. "It must be really bad driving around it on a day like this!"

"That's for sure," Jen agreed, heading out of the foyer toward her room. Zeke followed her through the large dining room to the circular lighthouse museum that occupied the bottom floor of the remodeled lighthouse tower. The eleven-year-old twins had helped design the museum, filling it with old photographs of the lighthouse, the nearby town of Mystic, Maine, and the Markham family, who had run the lighthouse for generations. Other memorabilia, such as old fishing tackle and some vintage foul-weather gear, were also on display.

Even though history wasn't one of Zeke's favorite subjects, digging into the history of the lighthouse had been fun. Besides, Aunt Bee knew everything there was to know about Mystic and its famous lighthouse. She had been the head librarian in town for many years. She claimed that she'd forgotten more facts than she remembered, but in Zeke's opinion she knew more than an encyclopedia.

At the back of the museum Uncle Cliff had installed a circular staircase. It wound past Jen's bedroom on the second floor and Zeke's on the third floor, all the way to the top platform of the lighthouse.

Jen went to her room, while Zeke climbed the extra flight to his. Jen had decorated her room with posters of athletes and a few of cats. In her usual style, none of the posters was hanging straight. In fact, they looked as if she had thrown them at the walls, sending them every which way. Zeke's posters of sailboats and *Star Wars* movies marched across his walls in a perfect line.

Zeke draped his wet clothes over the back of his desk chair to dry. He pulled on a green sweatshirt and gray sweatpants, and finally felt warm and dry. As he rubbed more water out of his dark, wavy hair, he peered out his window that overlooked the Atlantic Ocean. The second window in his room faced the bay.

The howling wind whipped the water below into white froth. Zeke shivered even though he wasn't cold. Sometimes the force of the stormy ocean gave him chills. *I wouldn't want to be out there in a boat*, he thought. Though he loved sailing and swimming, he knew how dangerous the ocean could be, especially in this weather.

His hair felt fairly dry, and after running his fingers through it, he rushed back down to Jen's room. When she opened her door, he saw that she had left her wet clothes in a soggy pile in the middle of the floor. Typical Jen. But he knew better than to say anything about it.

As they hurried through the dining room, the lights flickered. The twins looked at each other, waiting for the inevitable to happen, but the lights stayed on.

Zeke groaned. "I just know it. We're going to lose power."

They continued through the parlor and joined Aunt Bee in the foyer. She took one look at them and smiled. "You two look like mice on a sinking ship. Why so glum?" Then she held up her hand for silence as Jen and Zeke started in about the rain and being cooped up and having no electricity. "Forget I asked," she said with a laugh. "It's not the end of the world. Maybe we won't lose power after all—"

As though on cue, thunder crackled close by. The lights flickered, then went out. The thick gray clouds outside blocked all the sunlight. With the lights off, it was so dark it felt like midnight to the twins, even though it was only three o'clock in the afternoon.

Jen heard the scrape of a match, and Aunt Bee's face reappeared, glowing in the soft light of one of the oil lamps. She adjusted the wick and grinned at them.

"The adventure begins," she said, lighting two more lamps. "Could you two prepare the other three rooms while I deliver these lights to our resting guests?"

Zeke snapped on a flashlight as Aunt Bee left the foyer, guided by her flickering lamp. The twins headed toward the front stairs. Linens and towels were kept in the bottom drawer of the dresser in each room. The quilts, sheets, and towels were coordinated to match each room's unique floral theme. It made preparing the rooms a lot easier.

They had just mounted the first step when Zeke stopped. "Did you hear that?" he whispered hoarsely.

"Hear what? It's probably just the wind blowing something around outside."

Zeke gripped her arm. "Shhhhh!"

"I don't hear anything." But as soon as the words were out of her mouth, Jen heard a strange thump. There was no way the wind could make a noise like that *inside* the B&B.

The twins stared at each other with wide eyes,

and Jen's heart started to hammer. "What was that?"

"It came from the parlor," answered Zeke.

"It's probably just Woofer," Jen said.

Zeke shook his head and aimed his flashlight toward the check-in counter. Woofer, their Old English sheepdog, lay beside it with his head resting on his paws. Slinky, their huge Maine coon cat, was curled up on top of the dog. It was their favorite way to nap.

Another dull thump came from the parlor.

Jen grabbed the light out of Zeke's hand and started to tiptoe in that direction. Zeke had no choice but to follow his sister since she had control of the flashlight.

They rounded the corner. The parlor piano and furniture looked like shadowy lumps—or crouching monsters. Then, in a nearly blinding flash of lightning, followed immediately by the crack of thunder, the twins saw a girl standing by the wall, her pale face staring back at them. The room went dark again. By the time Jen swerved the flashlight to the spot where the girl had stood along the wall, the girl was gone!

Double Take

"Did you see that?" Jen gasped. Then she gave a little shriek as something wound around her ankles. It took her a second to realize it wasn't a ghostly hand, but Slinky.

"See what?" asked Zeke.

"That girl! She—she looked like a ghost."

"It must have been a trick of the light," Zeke said, not sounding too sure of himself.

"So you *did* see her?"

Reluctantly, Zeke nodded until he realized it was too dark for his sister to see him. "I saw her, but only for a second."

"She disappeared into thin air. Did you see her face?" Jen asked, her voice still low.

"Yup," Zeke said, swallowing hard. "She didn't look too happy."

"An angry ghost."

Zeke wished his sister hadn't said that. After all, they had heard strange noises in the lighthouse tower before—soft laughter, the creak of floorboards, odd whistling. There was even an old legend in town about a ghost who blew out the flame in the lighthouse so that ships would wreck on the rocks below. Even though that story was good for a few chills, they'd never actually seen or heard anything menacing. Until now.

"Maybe we just imagined it," Zeke said.

"No way," Jen protested, a shiver trickling up her spine. "I saw her. She looked right at me."

Zeke tugged his sister's arm. "Come on, we have to get the rooms ready."

Reluctantly, Jen let her brother lead her upstairs. Had she really seen a ghost? She couldn't think about anything else as they checked the Rose Room, making sure the bed was neatly made and the bathroom was in order, with pink towels hanging evenly on the rack. Aunt Bee liked to call the B&B her "flower-filled hive" because of all the floral patterns everywhere—on pillows, wallpaper, lampshades, and curtains. When Zeke tried to explain to her that a hive was full of honey, not flowers, Aunt Bee had simply said that at sixty-two years old she could fill her hive with flowers if she wanted to. After all, she'd added, honey was made from flowers, and wasn't she a "Bee"?

By the time they got to the room they called the Hibiscus Hideaway, the storm had gotten worse. It was slamming loose branches against the windows and pushing cold air through every crack, creating eerie moans and whistles. When they finished preparing the Hibiscus Hideaway, they moved downstairs to the Violet Valley, which was just off the foyer. This was Jen's favorite guest room because it was decorated in purple: purple flowered wallpaper, purple striped curtains, a purple painted dresser— even the towels in the bathroom were purple. Purple was Jen's favorite color.

When they came out of the room, Aunt Bee was busy at the check-in counter. Before her stood a middle-aged couple in raincoats that dripped water on the floor around them. The tall man looked like a giant next to the short, round woman with him. The woman sneezed three times in a row, then rummaged through her large red canvas handbag and retrieved a crumpled tissue.

Aunt Bee asked, "Have you had that cold long, Mrs. Snyder?"

"Excuse me?" Mrs. Snyder said, cupping a hand to her ear.

"How long have you been sick?" Aunt Bee asked, raising her voice above the storm.

"Oh, not long. A day or two," Mrs. Snyder nearly shouted back. "It's just the sniffles."

As the twins approached, Aunt Bee introduced them to the new guests.

"Professor Snyder is writing a book about Maine," Aunt Bee explained.

Professor Snyder looked down at them through gold-rimmed glasses and smiled under his salt-and-pepper mustache. "It's been very interesting so far. I'm especially looking forward to the Mystic bicentennial celebration."

"But it'll get canceled because of the storm," Jen blurted out.

The professor's face fell. "I've come all this way."

Aunt Bee nodded. "I'm afraid Jen is right. The storm has also caused two couples to cancel their reservations with us."

The professor looked even more upset. "Oh, no."

"You're welcome to cancel your reservation," Aunt Bee offered. "I'd certainly understand."

"No, no, we've come this far," Professor Snyder said reluctantly.

"Then just sign in here," Aunt Bee said as she pointed to the registration book, "and then the twins will help you to your room."

Jen reached for Mrs. Snyder's overnight bag, which was also made of red canvas, and hefted it in her right hand.

"These people have already checked in?" the professor asked, his pen poised above the registration book.

"That's right, Lenore Mills and her daughter," Aunt Bee confirmed, peering at the open book. "They're upstairs, but you'll be meeting them at dinner."

Professor Snyder beamed. "How delightful."

As Zeke started to reach for his suitcase, the professor snatched it. "This is too heavy for you, young man. It's full of my research books. Just point the way and I'll take care of it."

Zeke felt his face burn. He knew he could carry the bag. But he was sure the professor wouldn't appreciate his wrestling the suitcase away from him, so Zeke simply led the couple to the Violet Valley.

Jen set Mrs. Snyder's suitcase on the bench at the foot of the bed as both Snyders admired the room decor. Aunt Bee, Uncle Cliff, and the twins had put a lot of thought into planning everything about the B&B, from the artwork on the walls to the size of the dining room table.

Professor Snyder carefully placed his oversized suitcase against the wall and tested the bed for firmness. He nodded with approval. "This will do just fine," he said. He handed each of the twins a crisp dollar bill and closed the door on their backs.

The twins joined their aunt at the check-in counter just as the front door opened and another guest stepped in. She tried to shut the door behind her but the wind pushed back and for a second it looked as if the wind might win.

With a loud "Oof," the woman shoved the door closed. "Nice weather," she commented with a wry grin as she approached. "And no electricity," she added, noting the oil lamp on the counter and the flashlight in Zeke's hand.

"Just pretend you've stepped back in time," Aunt Bee suggested, "and you'll have a marvelous time."

The woman shivered. "How delightful. I always wondered what it would be like to live in the 1800s."

She patted her straight black hair as if to make sure the wind hadn't blown it away. It was surprisingly neat and hung down to her shoulders. Her narrow face had at first looked serious, but as soon as she smiled, her eyes lit up like twinkling stars.

Aunt Bee stared openly at the newest guest until even Jen noticed her staring and coughed. Aunt Bee laughed and focused on the registration process. "I'm sorry, Mrs. Barr," she said. "But you look so familiar to me."

"I just have one of those faces that looks familiar, that's all. And please, call me Esther."

"I'm sure that's it," Aunt Bee said lightly. "Now, if you'll just sign in, Zeke will show you to the Rose Room on the second floor."

Just as Zeke was about to head up the stairs with Esther Barr, the front door blew open and a tall man rushed in, slamming the door shut behind him. Jen stared at him. Even though she didn't watch much TV, she recognized him immediately. It was Jaspar Westcombe, the famous television reporter who did special assignments for the national news. Jen remembered that his last special had been about an Egyptian tomb filled with gold statues. She would know his suntanned, chiseled face anywhere. Even in the storm, his blond hair was smooth and slicked back—just like on TV. She was so amazed that she didn't notice the way he did a double take when he spied Esther standing at the foot of the stairs. But Zeke did. He also saw that Esther quickly turned away from the reporter with a look of panic on her face and rushed up the stairs.

3

The Dark Lighthouse

Jen tried not to stare as Jaspar Westcombe introduced himself to Aunt Bee.

"Are you on assignment?" Jen asked, inching closer.

Jaspar laughed. "Oh, no. I'm just here for a relaxing weekend. I've been working too hard and I need some R&R—rest and relaxation."

"That's what we're here for," Aunt Bee sang out. "R&R at the B&B."

Jen took one of the reporter's bags and led him upstairs to his room.

"You're in the Hibiscus Hideaway," she said as she aimed her flashlight at the floor so he wouldn't trip. When she opened the door to his room, he whistled in appreciation. The best part of this room was a live hibiscus bush with three orange blooms on it in an enormous pale green ceramic pot. The blossoms were closing up a bit, but they were still pretty and fragrant.

"This is great," he said. "Thanks for your help." He handed Jen a two-dollar tip.

Jen met Zeke at the top of the stairs and they headed down together. She told him about their famous guest.

Then Zeke told her about Esther Barr's reaction to seeing Jaspar Westcombe enter the foyer. "As soon as she saw him, she became nervous and edgy."

"She even acted weird when Aunt Bee said she looked familiar," Jen said. She was about to say more, but the grandfather clock in the dining room bonged six times, cutting her off. Aunt Bee called to them from the kitchen. She needed their help in preparing a light supper of clam chowder and steaming-hot biscuits for the guests. Even though there was no electricity for lights or to pump up the water from the well, they could still cook because Aunt Bee had a gas oven and a gas-powered refrigerator. Because the electricity went out so easily during a storm, she had switched to gas so she could still feed her guests.

When the meal was ready, Zeke knocked on all the doors and told the guests that the food would be left on the sideboard in the dining room for a couple of hours, being kept warm with a Sterno food heater. He invited them to help themselves when they got hungry. When he returned to the dining room, he found Jen and Aunt Bee already eating, so he joined them. He dug into his chowder. No doubt about it, Aunt Bee was the best cook in Mystic.

After they ate, the twins retreated to Jen's room to finish a game of Monopoly they'd been playing earlier.

"I am the champion!" Zeke crowed when he finally bankrupted Jen.

Jen grinned. "Just wait till next time, Mr. Champion. I have a whole new strategy planned."

Zeke laughed. "You always say that and you always lose. Come on, Aunt Bee probably wants us to wash the dishes."

When they got downstairs, they were surprised to see the dining room and kitchen already spotless.

"There you are," Aunt Bee said, swishing her long gray braid out of the way as she ran a towel over the counter one last time. "Hiding on me?"

"No!" Jen exclaimed. "We were in my room, playing—"

"I was only teasing," Aunt Bee said with a laugh. "The guests finished early, so I cleaned up without you. But I did save the best job. Normally I'd say you should wait till it stops raining, but I don't think that's going to happen for awhile. If you take out the garbage now, you won't have to worry about it again till Monday. By then, the storm should have blown itself out."

The twins each lugged one heavy bag out the back door of the kitchen. In the beating rain, they hurried to the side of the B&B where they kept the trash bins. Jen clenched her teeth, feeling the cold water trickle under her hood.

After they'd dumped their load, they raced around to the front of the building. Jen suddenly stopped and looked up at the B&B, trying to protect her eyes from the slashing rain. The glimmer of oil lamps shone from several windows, but the lighthouse tower was dark. Aunt Bee usually kept the electric lamp at the top of the lighthouse lit, even though it wasn't an official lighthouse anymore. She did it for the historical feel it gave the B&B, she said. And even though there were electronic sounding systems to warn ships and boats away from the dangerous rocks and cliffs, local fishermen said they loved to see the lighthouse when they were out late. It gave them a sense of comfort and welcome as they headed home in their boats.

Now with the power out, the lighthouse looked eerie. Jen shivered, imagining what it must have been like in the old days, trying to find the safe harbor in a storm without a beacon from the lighthouse. One wrong turn and the ship would crash against the rocks.

When they got inside, Jen told Zeke how creepy she thought the dark lighthouse would have been in the old days.

"But the light wasn't run by electricity back then," Zeke reminded her. "It was the lighthouse keeper's job to make sure the oil lamp didn't burn out."

"What if the lighthouse keeper was sick or something?"

Zeke shrugged. "Maybe he had an assistant." He looked around. The B&B was quiet. "I guess Aunt Bee went to bed," he commented.

"Everyone else must be asleep, too," Jen whispered as they peeled off their coats and hung them up on the pegs near the front door.

Zeke yawned as he flicked on the small flashlight he'd kept in his pocket. "I guess I'll go to bed, too. I can't work on the computer, I can't watch TV, and I can't—"

"Oh, stop complaining," Jen interrupted. "I have a great idea."

Zeke looked at his twin doubtfully. Jen wasn't known for her great ideas. "What is it?"

"Let's go look for the ghost! Come on," Jen urged,

her blue eyes flashing. "It'll be fun."

"Looking for a ghost doesn't sound like fun to me. It sounds crazy."

"Then I'm going alone," Jen said, starting off through the dimly lit foyer.

"Wait." The beam from the flashlight bobbed on the floor ahead of Zeke as he caught up. "I'll go with you."

Silently, they searched the foyer, then the parlor and the dining room.

"Forget it," Zeke said. "There's no ghost. We must have imagined it before." As the words left his mouth, they heard a crash in the kitchen.

Jen raced forward with Zeke following two feet behind her. He aimed the flashlight around the room. Nothing.

Jen tugged on his sleeve and pointed to the open pantry. "In there!" she whispered excitedly.

Tiptoeing, hearts slamming against their ribs, they nervously made their way to the opening in the pantry. Taking a deep breath, Zeke shined his light in.

The beam fell on a pale, shimmering figure.

4

Secret Passages

Zeke dropped the flashlight and it blinked and went out. The pantry was pitch-black. Jen dove for the last place she had seen the flashlight. Other hands were reaching around at the same time. Their fingers got tangled. Finally Zeke got hold of the flashlight and switched it on.

The pale girl hadn't disappeared. She stood there, glaring at them. And in the glow of the flashlight, they could see that she had long, reddish-brown hair. "Don't shine that light in my eyes," she said crossly.

Zeke lowered the beam. "Who are you?"

"Karen Mills. I'm staying here with my mom. Who are you?"

"Jen and Zeke. We live here," Jen answered. "What are you doing?"

The girl's gaze flitted around the dark pantry. "I—

uh—was looking for something to eat."

Jen and Zeke glanced at each other.

"I'm not hungry anymore," Karen said, edging by them to get out of the pantry. "I'll see you later." With that she sprinted out of the kitchen and the twins heard her footsteps fade quickly.

"What was she doing here?" Jen wondered aloud. "I'm sure she wasn't looking for food."

Zeke silently agreed with his sister. He looked at the cans of stewed tomatoes and jars of homegrown string beans. "Something about her is so familiar," Zeke added as he examined the wall of pantry shelves where Karen had been standing. What had she been looking for?

Finally he gave up the search. Nothing looked out of the ordinary or out of place. They headed toward their bedrooms.

Zeke shrugged his shoulders. "There's something strange about Karen."

Jen yawned. "Like what?"

As they walked through the lighthouse museum, Jen headed straight for the circular stairs. But Zeke stood in the museum, sweeping the beam of light from his flashlight across the wall of old photographs. His light finally settled on one yellowed photograph in its original silver frame.

"Look," he called to Jen.

She came beside him and looked at the photograph. She remembered finding the photo in an old trunk in the attic. It was a picture of a young girl standing in front of a Christmas tree, holding a teddy bear in her arms. Jen's blood froze in her veins. "That's—that's her! That's Karen Mills!"

Zeke peered at the inscription etched in the silver frame. "No, it's Catherine Markham, the daughter of the original lighthouse keeper. That must have been about 1900."

"But they could be identical twins!"

Zeke agreed. "I knew she looked familiar. But this is really spooky."

Jen shivered. "Karen's not a ghost, though. Right?"

"When she brushed past us as she left the pantry, she didn't feel like a ghost," Zeke said. "She felt warm and solid like a human being."

"We have to find out what's going on," Jen said, forgetting how tired she'd felt only minutes before.

Zeke checked his watch. "It's too late now."

"It's only ten o'clock!" Jen protested, glancing over his shoulder at the glowing dial.

"Everyone's already in bed. If we wake up a guest Aunt Bee won't be too thrilled. We'll just have to start first thing tomorrow."

Jen woke up Saturday morning to the sounds of not-so-distant thunder, rain pelting against her windows, and storm-driven waves crashing into the cliff below. She snuggled deeper under her quilt. This was a perfect day to stay cuddled up with a good book.

She suddenly sprang out of bed. How could she lie there when there was a ghostly look-alike eating breakfast downstairs? She threw on a wrinkled T-shirt and a pair of sweatpants. Then she ran her fingers through her hair, pushed her feet into her favorite pair of old sneakers, and rushed down to the dining room.

Zeke was already there, helping Aunt Bee set up the coffee and juice table and arranging the fresh rolls and muffins on the dining room table. A warm, cheery fire roared in the fireplace. Woofer was sleeping on the small rug in front of the hearth, but Slinky was nowhere to be seen. Nor had the cat slept with Jen the previous night, which was unusual. Unease rippled through her, but she shrugged it off. Slinky was smarter than most humans and knew how to stay out of trouble. Usually.

Jen put out the homemade jams and jellies and a dish of butter. The muffins smelled awesome; her favorite kind was banana macadamia nut. As soon as everything was set up, she grabbed one, along with a glass of orange juice, and settled at the dining room table as the guests trickled in.

Aunt Bee greeted each person by name, explaining the variety of freshly baked muffins and rolls. The twins sat side by side, inspecting the guests as they made their breakfast choices. At one point Jen nudged Zeke in the ribs. "Look at that," she whispered.

Zeke turned to see Jaspar Westcombe heading straight for Esther Barr, who was choosing a muffin. When Jaspar tapped her to get her attention, she looked up, startled. *Was that a flash of fear in her eyes?* Jen wondered.

Aunt Bee clapped her hands for attention. "I'm so sorry about the electricity still being out. It's back on in town, but if the storm continues, it may go out again. Unfortunately, we're a ways out of town and always the last ones to get power restored. I'm so sorry."

"It's delightful," Esther said, waving her hand. "It makes me feel like I'm living long ago."

Zeke noticed that as she talked, Esther edged away from Jaspar and sat down at the table between Jen and a thin, pale woman whose hair was the same reddish-brown color as Karen Mills's hair. Karen sat on the other side of the thin woman—she was obviously Karen's mother. Esther nervously touched a hand to her bangs, brushing a lock away from her face. Now there was no way for Jaspar to get to her without being rude or overly obvious. But why was the investigative reporter chasing her?

"How on earth did you bake these delicious goodies?" Mrs. Snyder asked. She and her husband had come in, filled their plates, and settled on the other side of Karen Mills.

Aunt Bee smiled at them in the candlelight. "I had a gas oven and refrigerator installed after the last big storm. We won't run out of food here. And I'm planning on serving all three meals for anyone interested, since getting into town will be a rather wet adventure. Even if you drive, you'll have to park and walk to the shops. You're sure to get soaked. I do have extra umbrellas for any brave souls, however. . . ."

Aunt Bee continued with her morning speech while Jen zoned out. She'd heard it all before. When all the guests had helped themselves, Aunt Bee made a small plate for herself and joined the others around the large dining room table. Aunt Bee liked her guests to mingle, so she served all the meals family-style at one large table. She looked around as she always did, making sure everyone had everything they needed. Staring at Karen Mills, she said, "Did you know you look remarkably like a girl in one of the photos in the lighthouse museum?"

Karen's mother laughed lightly. "I noticed that when I was wandering around yesterday. As a matter of fact, Catherine Markham is my great-great-aunt. Karen has her old diary."

"Really?" asked Professor Snyder. "How interesting. I would love to see it. It would be a marvelous research source for my book."

"What, dear?" Mrs. Snyder said. "Did you say something?"

Professor Snyder raised his voice. "Nothing, dear."

"Why don't you tell everyone about it?" Mrs. Mills suggested to her scowling daughter.

"It's not that interesting," Karen said curtly, crossing her arms.

Mrs. Mills chuckled. "She's being modest. Karen has read it more than ten times." She lowered her voice. "The diary even talks about secret passageways and hidden rooms in this old place."

Jen and Zeke looked at each other. *Secret passages!*

"I've heard those rumors," Aunt Bee said. "But I've been living here for years and I haven't found anything of the sort, I'm sorry to say. Every square foot is pretty well accounted for."

"That's what I said," Mrs. Mills remarked, looking at her daughter. "But she's been dying to visit the lighthouse ever since she first read the old diary. I thought this bicentennial celebration would be a good time to come."

"How sad that most of the events will be canceled because of the weather and the power failure," Aunt Bee said. "But I'd be happy to take anyone on a tour of our historic town this weekend, and certainly of the B&B as well."

"That would be fun. Maybe we'll find old Aunt Catherine's treasure," Mrs. Mills said, grinning at her daughter.

At these words, Karen gave her mother a dark glare.

"Treasure?" Jen piped in. "What treasure?"

"Never mind," Karen said before her mother could open her mouth. "There is no treasure."

Jen caught Zeke's eye and knew what he was thinking. *Karen is lying!* Now they knew why she was poking around in the pantry.

5

Up to Something

Esther Barr clapped her hands. "A treasure! How perfect."

"There is no treasure," Karen insisted.

"Oh, I'm sure there must be," Esther said. Her straight black hair swung from side to side. "It's just what I was hoping for."

"Why?" Zeke asked.

Esther looked startled. "Oh, no reason. Just my silly imagination getting away from me."

"A lighthouse treasure, now that's interesting," Jaspar said. Jen noticed a gleam in his eyes. A moment later, he excused himself. As he walked out of the dining room, Jen saw him pull a cell phone out of his jacket pocket.

Professor Snyder was chuckling softly. "A treasure," he finally said. "What a wonderful fantasy.

Unfortunately, it is completely impossible."

"Why is it impossible?" Karen demanded.

Jen noticed that Karen sounded disappointed even though she'd just insisted that there wasn't a treasure.

"As you all know, I'm writing a book on Maine, and I have done a great deal of research on the small coastal towns like Mystic. Believe me, there is no mention of a treasure left by some pirate. Mystic wasn't even a very important port, which is why this lighthouse stopped being used quite early."

"That's correct," Aunt Bee agreed, beginning to clear away the dishes. Jen and Zeke hopped up to help. "My husband and I had to put electricity in the lighthouse ourselves."

"What did they use before that?" Mrs. Mills asked.

Professor Snyder cleared his throat and began speaking as though he were giving a lecture to a room full of students. "Before electricity, lighthouses used whale oil lamps, which the lighthouse keeper had to keep filled. Some lights were stationary and didn't revolve. Others were wound up with a clockwork mechanism so that the lights turned in circles."

"What if the keeper forgot to fill the oil lamps?" Jen asked.

The professor turned to her, his gray eyebrows pressing low over his eyes. "Then ships crashed against the shore and lives were lost."

Jen shuddered and the dishes in her arms wobbled. Quickly she brought them into the kitchen. *Ships sank and lives were lost.*

Zeke came up behind her with an empty pitcher.

Jen whirled around. "Jeez, don't sneak up on me like that."

"Why are you so jumpy?"

"I was just thinking about all those poor sailors looking for the light after long, long days at sea, then not seeing the dangerous rocks and cliffs till they had crashed into them."

"It's like the town legend about the ghost who blew out the lamps, leaving the lighthouse dark," Zeke mused.

"And now the lighthouse is dark again," Jen said, feeling an odd fear tightening her throat. "Just like long ago. . . ." She let her voice trail off.

For a second, Zeke stood spellbound. Then he shook himself. "You should be a writer," he said, chuckling. He headed out of the kitchen.

Jen filled a pot of water from the bucket by the back door. The water was from the outside well. She turned on the gas burner, using a match to ignite the flame, and then placed the pot on the stove. She stood by the stove, waiting for the water to warm up so that she could wash the dishes. Zeke took his time clearing away the rest of the breakfast dishes as the guests made plans for the day.

"Karen and I are going into town," Lenore Mills said, still sipping her coffee.

"But it's raining," Karen protested.

Mrs. Mills laughed. "I don't think you'll melt from a little rain."

"It's more than a little," Karen grumbled.

"Excuse me?" Mrs. Snyder said loudly, pointing to her ear. "I didn't quite catch that."

"Never mind," Professor Snyder said to his wife. He stood up and his wife followed suit. "I have some work to do in my room," he told the others.

"I'll just relax in the parlor," Mrs. Snyder said, digging a paperback book out of her huge red purse.

After they left, Esther rose gracefully. "I'm just going to mosey around the old place, if you don't mind. This is such a fascinating setting." With that, she strolled out of the dining room, looking around with interest at the furniture, the pictures on the walls, and the views from the windows.

Zeke carried his load into the kitchen, where the water had finally heated and Jen was now washing the dishes. She flung soap suds at him.

Aunt Bee appeared at that moment and put her

hands on her hips. "I saw that."

Jen tried to defend herself, but she knew her aunt wasn't really angry. In fact, Jen reasoned, the one good suds fight they'd had last summer, Aunt Bee had started!

"Zeke, get me the scissors from the front desk, please," Aunt Bee asked.

Zeke jogged through the dining room and into the foyer. He stopped in his tracks when he heard Esther Barr's voice. As he neared the desk, Esther's silky voice became louder and louder, and Zeke realized she must be just down the hall near the Daffodil Den. He strained his ears, trying to listen.

". . . do anything to get that treasure. Absolutely anything . . . hunt for it night and day, and do whatever is necessary to find it. . . ."

Zeke gulped. He grabbed the scissors and hurried back to the kitchen.

As soon as Aunt Bee left, he quickly told Jen what he'd overheard. Her eyes widened. "I knew there was something suspicious about her. Who was she talking to?"

"I don't know. I didn't hear another voice. Maybe she has a cell phone."

Jen wiped the last dish and placed it on the rack to dry. "Come on, let's see if she's still talking."

As they made their way into the dining room,

they heard Mrs. Mills set down her coffee cup at the far end of the room and say, "Let's go, honey."

"Uh, I don't feel so hot, Mom," Karen said.

Zeke and Jen backtracked a few steps into the museum and peeked around the door.

Karen was making a face that, even in the spotty lighting, Jen recognized immediately as a "faking being sick" face. She'd tried it a few times herself.

Mrs. Mills must have seen it before, too, because she narrowed her eyes at her daughter. "Are you sure?"

"The town is quite lovely," Aunt Bee added as she walked into the dining room.

Karen looked even sicker. "I'm sure it is. I'll just go lie down."

With a shrug of defeat, Mrs. Mills pulled on a lavender raincoat. Jen loved the color, and saw that it looked great with Mrs. Mills's pale complexion and pretty hair. Then the twins lost sight of her as she headed into the foyer with Aunt Bee.

Now the dining room was empty. Karen looked around nervously, not noticing Jen and Zeke watching her from behind the museum door. She picked up a flashlight. Instead of heading in the direction of her room, she tiptoed into the kitchen.

"She's up to something," Jen hissed. She stepped stealthily after Karen, Zeke close behind. They moved silently into the kitchen. Empty. Jen pointed to the pantry and put a finger over her lips. Zeke nodded. They were sure they would find Karen where they had found her last night. Taking care to move as quietly as possible, they slid into the pantry.

Jen gasped. Karen had disappeared!

6

A Valuable Secret

"I knew it!" Jen exclaimed, forgetting to keep her voice down. "She *is* a ghost!"

Zeke was examining the shelves as he had last night. He pressed and tugged and jiggled them. "You're nuts, you know that?" he said as he continued to work. "Karen is *not* a ghost. There has to be a logical explanation for this. Get me a flashlight."

For once, Jen didn't argue. She shone the light for him. Suddenly, he went still and cocked his head.

"Hear that?"

Jen strained her ears. Yes! It was a muffled meowing sound. "Hey, that's Slinky, and it sounds as if she's behind the wall!"

Zeke resumed his inspection of the shelves and the wall, pressing and poking everywhere. "Hey, shine the light over here. See the gap?"

"Maybe it's a hidden door," Jen said, tingling with excitement.

Zeke pushed the canned tomatoes out of the way and ran his fingers along the edge of the narrow slit. Nothing.

"Try again," Jen urged.

Concentrating, Zeke pressed harder, hoping he wouldn't get a splinter from the old wood. Suddenly, an entire three-foot-wide section of the wall swung backward, leaving a black hole.

Slinky streaked out, covered with dust.

Jen lunged for the cat, but Slinky disappeared around the corner faster than a lightning bolt.

"How long has she been back there?" Jen wondered out loud. "She didn't sleep with me, so she must have been stuck back there all night."

Zeke wasn't listening. "A secret tunnel!"

Jen whirled around and peered into the dark gap. Without pausing she lunged forward, eager to see what was inside.

Zeke pulled her back. "Be careful," he said. "You don't know what's back there."

"Obviously Karen went in here. Come on." She stepped lightly into the dark, narrow passage. Almost immediately they came upon a staircase leading down. Jen flashed her light down the stairs, but the steps seemed to go on forever. She wasn't so eager anymore.

Zeke gave her a nudge. "Well? Are you going or not?"

"I guess so." Taking a deep breath, as though it might be her last, Jen started down.

Zeke stayed close behind, counting the steps as they went. When the stairs didn't stop at fifteen, the way the stairs into the basement did, he realized they were going to a level *below* the basement.

"It's cold down here," Jen said, shivering.

Zeke touched the wall. "This passageway was carved out of stone."

"The steps are wood," Jen commented. "And they're pretty dusty and dirty. But these footprints look like they were made recently."

"They must be Karen's," Zeke said.

At last they reached the bottom of the stairs.

"I feel like a character in a fairy tale or a fantasy story," Jen whispered. Ahead of them were two openings. She shined the light to the left. "Those stairs go up." Aiming the flashlight forward she saw that the ground was level. "Let's go this way."

They crept along. Zeke tried not to think about the rough walls closing in on him, or the fact that they were at least twenty feet underground. The air was musty, but every once in a while he swore he felt a slight breeze that smelled of fresh air and salt water. The tunnel twisted and turned, completely disorienting him. Soon they came to a three-way fork in the tunnel. To the right they saw another staircase leading down. The paths straight ahead and to the left looked like continuous tunnels.

"Which way did Karen go?" Jen asked.

As if to answer her question, they heard a soft sneeze. Jen motioned straight ahead with her flashlight and they hurried on. Just around a bend the light fell on Karen, who was trying to hold back another sneeze. When she saw them, she let the sneeze go.

"Gesundheit," Zeke said.

Karen frowned at them. "What are you two doing down here?"

"We followed you," Jen explained. "We want to know why you're snooping around. And how did you find these tunnels?"

"I'm not snooping, just exploring," Karen said defensively.

"Well, you disappeared last night in the parlor," Jen replied. "The way you just took off made it look like snooping to me."

"Never mind," Zeke interrupted. "The point is that you found these secret tunnels, and now we've found you. But don't worry," he added hastily when he saw the worried look on Karen's face. "We won't tell anyone. Right, Jen?"

"Of course not," Jen snapped. Then she relaxed and her face cracked a small grin. "This is way too interesting to share."

Karen eyed the twins doubtfully for a long moment. "Okay, I'll tell you the truth. But you have to swear not to tell anyone."

Jen and Zeke nodded.

"It's true that I have Catherine Markham's diary," Karen went on. "That's how I found out about these secret tunnels. As soon as we got here yesterday, I started looking around. That's it."

"That's it?" Jen repeated doubtfully.

"What about the treasure?" Zeke pressed. "Is there one?"

Karen still looked worried.

"You can tell us," Jen said. "We'll help you find it."

"So far all I've found are three entrances into the tunnels: from the parlor, the pantry, and an empty guest room."

"Cool!" Jen exclaimed. "We've lived here for years and never even knew. I can't believe Aunt Bee never found the secret entrances."

"But is there really a treasure?" Zeke asked.

Karen shrugged. "I haven't found anything. One

of the passages at the second fork goes to a room with old shelves along the walls, like a storage room. The other passage goes down even deeper." She grinned shyly. "But I was too chicken to check it out. And this one comes straight here, as you know. I haven't found any gold or anything yet, though."

"Gold?" Jen said with a gasp.

"I doubt it." Karen took a deep breath as though she were making a hard decision. "I should probably tell you something else. Catherine's diary ended abruptly. This is her last entry." She closed her eyes and recited as though she were reading the words behind her eyelids. *"The mystery of the dark lighthouse is too awful to bear. If only I could confide in someone. But with so much wealth at stake, whom might I trust? Therefore, I must leave the truth for someone to find many years from now. Then all shall be discovered. I will hide the valuable secret as best I can, in case I need it someday. As always, X marks the spot to the left."*

"The dark lighthouse again," Zeke said with a shudder. He quickly told Karen the town legends about a ghost blowing out the lamps and making the lighthouse dark and dangerous. "I wonder what Catherine knew about it."

"Her secret obviously has something to do with the hidden treasure," Jen said, her voice squeaky with

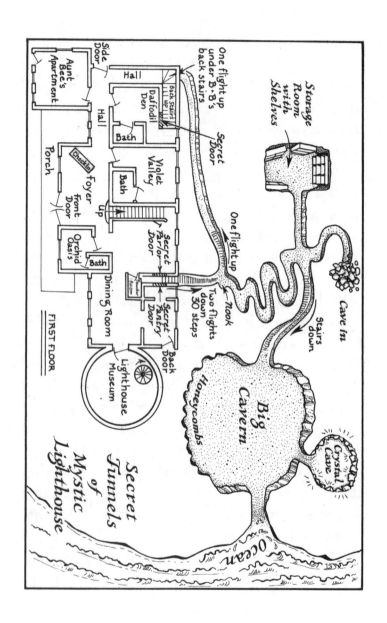

FIRST FLOOR

Secret Tunnels of Mystic Lighthouse

Side Door

Aunt Bee's Apartment

Hall

Hall

Daffodil Den

Bath

Back Stairs

One flight up under B+B's back stairs

Secret Door

Violet Valley

Bath

Checking

Foyer

Porch

Front Door

Up

Secret Parlor Door

Orchid Oasis

Bath

One flight up

Nook

Powder Room

Secret Pantry Door

Two flights down 30 steps

Dining Room

Back Door

Lighthouse Museum

Storage Room with Shelves

Cave In

Stairs down

Honeycombs

Big Cavern

Crystal Cave

Ocean

excitement. "We have to find the treasure to uncover her secret."

"And the only way to do that," Zeke added, "is to solve the clues that Catherine left in her diary."

"Well, we'd better hurry," Karen said sharply.

Jen looked at her. "Why?"

"I found a digging pick just beyond here."

"One of the picks they used to dig the tunnels?" Zeke asked.

Karen shook her head. "No. The pick wasn't there last night. There can only be one explanation for it."

"One of the other guests has found the tunnels and is looking for the treasure!" Jen and Zeke practically said in unison.

Karen nodded. "But who?"

X Marks the Spot

"Where's the pick?" Zeke asked.

Karen led them deeper into the tunnel, which ended suddenly.

"Looks like a cave-in," Jen said uneasily, eyeing the tumbled rocks and dirt blocking the passage. "I hope the rest of the tunnel doesn't collapse."

Karen agreed as she shone her light on the pick. Zeke crouched down to examine the dirty wooden handle and the sharp metal point.

"It looks old, but these shiny scratches show that it's been used recently against something hard, like these stone walls. The rocks scraped off the rust and dirt."

"So whose is it?" Karen asked.

"Beats me," Zeke admitted.

"Look at these footprints in the dust," Jen said.

She aimed her flashlight beyond the spot where they were standing.

"Those are mine," Karen said, pointing.

"But those aren't." Jen kept the light steady on a pair of larger footprints. "And there are Slinky's paw prints. Hey, what's that?" Something small and round sparkled in the dim light. Jen picked up the object and turned it over in her hand.

Zeke peered closely at it. "Weird. It's a button."

Karen stared at the sparkling sphere without saying anything.

"It's definitely a clue," Jen said, slipping the button into her pocket. "Someone came down here and lost it!"

Zeke held up three fingers. "So now we have the pick, the footprints, and the button."

"Come on," Karen said hastily as her flashlight flickered. "Let's get out of here. I think my flashlight is about to go dead."

The group hurried back along the tunnel and up the thirty steps to the short hall where the door into the pantry was still open.

"There's a door on that side, too," Karen explained, pointing to the opposite wall.

"From the parlor," said Jen. "That's how you

disappeared last night." Jen grinned. "We thought you were a ghost."

Karen smiled. "Maybe I am."

As soon as they stepped into the pantry, Zeke pulled the hidden door closed and an entire panel of shelves clicked back into place. It was completely camouflaged. If a person didn't know it was there, no way would he find it. They were on their way to the parlor to talk when Mrs. Mills pounced on them. Her raincoat was still zipped and water droplets glistened on the lavender fabric.

"There you are, Karen," she said. "I found the cutest store in town. I came all the way back here to drag you down there. We can get souvenirs. Come on."

Karen looked at the twins and shrugged. "Later, you guys."

Jen and Zeke nodded. They knew what she meant by *later*. Later they would try to sort out the clues and find the treasure.

The twins peeked into the parlor where Mrs. Snyder was sitting in the corner chair, thumbing through a book. Not wanting to disturb her or be over-heard, they settled into the two comfortable window chairs in the foyer.

"So if everyone here knows about the treasure and is probably interested in it," Zeke said quietly, "that means the pick could belong to any one of the guests."

Jen nodded glumly. "That doesn't help us at all."

"The footprints were pretty big so they probably belong to a man—Professor Snyder or Jaspar."

"But they were smudged, so they could actually belong to anyone."

Zeke frowned. "True. And we have a button with no idea of who lost it."

"The best we can do, then, is try to solve Catherine's riddle. Since Karen is the only person with the diary, we have a clue no one else has."

"*As always,*" Zeke recited, "*X marks the spot to the left.*"

"That's a big help," Jen said. "It sounds like something from a really bad pirate movie. 'X marks the spot to the left.'" They lounged around for the next hour, cozy in the chairs, when suddenly Jen bolted upright in her seat.

"What?" Zeke asked, sensing his sister's excitement.

Jen grabbed his arm. "Come on!" She raced through the parlor and into the small bathroom. Mrs. Snyder started to say something, but Jen quickly shut the door.

In a strained whisper, Jen said, "When we were refinishing the parlor and the bathroom a couple of years ago, I noticed something. Aunt Bee said to leave it because this wall is obviously part of the original old building." She pointed to the scarred wall behind the sink. "She thought it would add a little old-time charm. So," Jen continued more slowly as she lifted off the mirror from above the sink. "Look at this."

Zeke stared at a cross carved into the wall. It had been hidden by the hanging mirror. "What does a crooked cross have to do with anything?"

Jen widened her eyes at her brother. She tilted her head to the left. "Look at it like this!"

Zeke followed her example. "As always, X marks the spot to the left!" With his head tilted to the left, the crooked cross became a clear X on the wall. "And look." He pointed. Just to the left of the X was a knothole in the old wood. It, too, had been covered by the mirror. Zeke pulled his Swiss army knife out of his pocket. Very carefully, he prodded at the knothole. It didn't budge.

"Dig at it more," Jen suggested.

Zeke stuck the shiny blade of his knife along one edge of the hole. He pushed it in deeper. Then, very carefully, he twisted the knife.

"It moved!" Jen exclaimed.

Trying not to scratch the wall any more than necessary, Zeke pried his knife loose and the knothole popped out like a cork.

The twins peered into the small cavity left behind. Jen stuck two fingers into the hole and removed a folded yellowed piece of paper.

8

The Ghost of the Dark Lighthouse

Suddenly someone banged on the door. "What's going on in there?" called a voice. "Are you okay?"

Jen hastily hung up the mirror to cover the X and the hole in the wall. "It's Mrs. Snyder. Let's go."

Zeke opened the door and the twins stepped out. "We're fine," he said. "Just, uh, tightening up the bolts on the cabinet. It's all nice and sturdy now."

"Oh," Mrs. Snyder said, narrowing her eyes.

The twins were saved from any further questions by the arrival of Karen and her mother.

Jen grinned at Karen. "We were just about to play Monopoly. Want to come?"

"Monopoly?" Karen said, wrinkling her forehead. Zeke gave her a look.

"Oh!" Karen turned to her mother. "Can I go with them?"

Mrs. Mills sighed. "Fine, go have fun." She gave

Karen a hug and headed for the dining room, where Aunt Bee had left thermoses of hot coffee and cocoa and several mugs.

Karen followed Jen and Zeke through the foyer, down the hall, and around the corner.

"Wait till you see what we found," Zeke exclaimed as soon as they were out of sight near the back stairs, trying to keep his voice down.

Karen's eyes widened. "You found the treasure already?"

Jen giggled under her breath. "Not yet, but we may have found something." She carefully handed over the old, brittle piece of paper and explained where they had found it.

Her fingers trembling with excitement, Karen unfolded it. First she read it silently. Her face fell. *"When Christmas goes, it leaves behind what I know."*

Jen made a face. "Why can't it just say to look under the third floorboard in the foyer to find the gold?"

"When Christmas goes, it leaves behind what I know," Zeke repeated, nodding thoughtfully.

"What was that?" Karen suddenly whispered. "I just heard a creak, like a squeaky floorboard."

Zeke cocked his head to listen, but could only hear Mrs. Snyder coughing in the parlor and the storm steadily blowing against the B&B.

Jen tiptoed around the corner, but the hall was clear all the way into the foyer. "Nothing. Maybe it was the Ghost of the Dark Lighthouse."

"What are you talking about?" Zeke demanded.

"There's been so much talk of ghosts and dark lighthouses," Jen replied, "I thought I'd give her a name."

Karen saw the twins were just kidding around, and her shoulders eased. "I thought you were serious."

Jen laughed. "Oh, we've heard ghostly noises before, but I don't think there's anything to worry about."

Even so, all three of them were alert on their way upstairs to Karen's room, the Sunflower Studio. They'd decided she should hide the note there before they continued their search for the treasure. After looking around, Karen tucked the note far under the dresser. Then they made their way downstairs again.

"Let's ask Aunt Bee if she knows anything about the treasure," Zeke suggested.

"But you said you wouldn't tell anyone," Karen said, a look of panic on her face.

Jen patted her arm. "Don't worry. We won't tell her anything important. Besides, if Aunt Bee really thought there was a treasure hidden here somewhere, she'd probably help us hunt for it."

They looked for her in the parlor, but found only

Mrs. Snyder. "There you are. Tell me what you were *really* doing in the bathroom," Mrs. Snyder demanded.

But before they had to make up an excuse, someone dropped a heavy object somewhere in the B&B. Suddenly, Mrs. Snyder broke into one of her coughing and sneezing fits. At one point she sneezed with such force, her purse flew off her lap.

Trying not to laugh, Jen quickly picked it up for her. She wasn't prepared for the weight of the purse, and it slipped sideways in her hand, spilling a few items.

"Sorry," she apologized, handing Mrs. Snyder the large red bag and picking up a packet of tissues, a key chain, and a book. Jen turned over the book and just had time to glance at the cover before Mrs. Snyder snatched it out of her hand.

Mrs. Snyder shoved the book back into her purse. She immediately started blowing her nose again.

Jen figured this was a good time to escape, so with a quick good-bye, she led the others out of the parlor. As soon as they were out of earshot, she whispered, "Did you guys see the title of that book? It was something about searching for treasure. Do you think she's the one hunting in the tunnels?"

"Mrs. Snyder hangs out in the parlor all the time. When would she have time to hunt?" Zeke asked.

"We'd hear her blowing her nose in the tunnels,

for sure," Karen added with a giggle. "I noticed that sound carries easily from the B&B into the tunnels."

They found Aunt Bee painting on a large canvas in her room. So far the painting looked like globs of red, orange, and purple. But Jen knew her aunt would transform it into a vivid sunset or beautiful close-up of a flower by the time she was through.

"Oh, sure," Aunt Bee said, after Zeke explained what they wanted. "There are rumors of treasure in many small towns. But I've never found evidence to support the rumors here in Mystic."

"Where can we find out more?" Jen asked.

Aunt Bee thought a moment. "There's an old book called *A Villager's Thoughts on a Small Town,* which is all about Mystic in the old days. That's the only place I've seen any treasure mentioned in writing. Happy hunting," she called as they left.

"We should go to the library and check out that book. Maybe it'll give us a hint about the Christmas clue," Jen said doubtfully. "At least we'll get out of the house."

On the way to the front door, they spotted Esther behind the registration desk. When she saw them, she straightened abruptly, a blush of red staining her cheeks. Patting her hair, she said, "You startled me. I was looking for a pen."

Jen reached over and plucked one from a cup full of pens on top of the counter and handed it to her.

"Oh, thank you. I didn't see those there." The pen in one hand and a lantern in the other, she hurried off.

None of them was looking forward to sloshing through the cold rain, but once they were outside and walking briskly, it wasn't too bad. Zeke, of course, didn't really mind getting wet. Sailing and swimming were two of his favorite activities, but stomping through puddles wasn't quite the same.

About twenty minutes and several shortcuts later, as they were nearing the library in town, Karen nudged Jen. "Don't look now," she said under her breath, "but I think there's someone following us."

Jen casually stopped to look in a window at a display of shoes and glanced behind them. There was someone! It looked like a man, but she couldn't be sure without staring, and she didn't want to be too obvious. As they continued on their way, Jen glanced behind them every once in a while. The person in the gray raincoat was still tailing them.

They hurried on to the library, and when Jen checked behind them one last time before they went in, there was the gray figure, standing across the street pretending to tie a shoe. Shaking off a chill, she followed Zeke and Karen into the library.

They hunted the stacks for the book Aunt Bee had told them about. They finally found it in a distant corner.

"I don't think anyone's ever taken this book out," Karen said, sneezing from the dust.

Handling the old, musty book with his fingertips, Zeke flipped through it. It didn't take him long to find the passage about treasure. "This is all it says: *Unto this day, the rumor persists of a ghost who blows out the lanterns in the lighthouse tower. In the black of night, without the light to guide them safely, ships wreck upon the rocks, leaving their treasures to the hungry ocean. The rumor would have one believe that the Ghost of the Dark Lighthouse reaped the treasure from the sea and hid it somewhere in the lighthouse.*"

"So there *is* something known as the Ghost of the Dark Lighthouse," Jen said.

"And the treasure from all the shipwrecks must be somewhere," Zeke muttered, closing the book and replacing it on the shelf.

On the return walk, Jen kept a sharp lookout but never saw any sign of anyone following them. They got back to the B&B, toweled off, and headed to the dining room for some hot cocoa. As they sipped their drinks and munched on cookies, Zeke reviewed the clues they had already found. Finally, he said, "If only we could figure out the Christmas clue, maybe we'd have some answers."

Jen plunked some marshmallows into her mug. "I wonder what Christmas was like back then."

"Catherine never wrote much about it in her diary," Karen offered. She took a sip of cocoa. "She always made gifts for her parents, and they each gave her one present."

"Like the teddy bear in that old photo," Jen said absently. "I bet that was a Christmas gift."

Zeke snapped his fingers. "That's it!"

9

Stolen

"What's 'it'?" Jen asked.

"The Christmas photo. Come on, I have an idea." He raced into the museum, with Jen and Karen right behind him. *"When Christmas goes, it leaves behind what I know.* This is a long shot, but it's worth a try." He carefully lifted the silver-framed photograph of Catherine Markham off the wall and turned it over. The back of the photograph was covered with a piece of paper. Zeke carefully removed it and revealed two lines of writing on the back of the picture. Triumphantly, he showed it to them.

One line read: *Catherine—Christmas 1901.* The next line, written in different handwriting, read: *When the lighthouse is dark, the distant shore is the mark.*

"Another clue!" Karen exclaimed. "That's definitely Catherine's handwriting."

Zeke put the protective piece of paper back in place and rehung the picture on the wall. "I think we need to look at everything we've found so far. Let's look at all the clues and see if there's anything we missed."

"How will it help to look at the first clue when we already found the next one?" Jen asked.

"Maybe there was something else written on the note that we missed."

"Or something written on the back," Karen said, agreeing with Zeke.

Jen thought they were being too hopeful—after all, she had studied the note carefully—but she knew it'd be no use arguing with them. She followed them up the stairs to the Sunflower Studio, where Karen had hidden the paper.

Karen opened the door to her room and gasped. "Oh, no!"

Zeke looked around at the mess. The beds were completely unmade and clothes lay scattered all around. All the drawers in the dresser stood open. Nothing looked broken or damaged in any way, but it would still take some time to straighten up. Obviously someone had been looking for something—probably Catherine's diary. Since Mrs. Mills had mentioned the diary and the treasure together, someone must have thought they'd be able to find the treasure if they had the diary. Luckily, Karen had left the diary at home.

"Your mom didn't do this, right?" Zeke asked, just to be sure.

Karen looked at him as if he were crazy. "No way. She hasn't seen this yet or we would have heard her yelling. And if I don't hurry and clean it up, she'll know we're up to something. Then she'll make me tell her what's going on."

"Then we'd better clean it up before she gets back," Zeke said.

Working together at top speed, it only took the three of them a few minutes to sort through the mess and put everything back in order. Finally finished, the twins settled on the edge of the bed while Karen poked under the dresser for the paper she'd hidden there, which was why they'd come up here in the first place. Then she lay her face sideways on the floor and stared under the piece of furniture.

"It's gone!"

"What?" Zeke exclaimed, getting on his hands and knees to look. Sure enough, the paper was gone. So the person had found the clue instead of the diary—but the clue was even more important. He jumped to his feet. "The second clue!" He ran all the way to the museum and Jen and Karen followed not far behind.

They whipped into the museum and stumbled to a halt in front of the space where the Christmas photograph had hung just moments before. The photograph was gone!

10

Help Me!

"Someone stole the clues right out from under our noses," Karen said hoarsely.

"That means someone is watching every move we make," Jen said, warily looking around. "They're figuring out the clues just after we are. But maybe now they're ahead of us and they'll find the treasure first."

Aunt Bee popped her head through the doorway. "Time to get lunch ready!"

Zeke pointed to the empty spot on the wall. "One of the old photos is missing," he told his aunt.

Aunt Bee frowned. "How strange." Then she brightened. "But I'm sure it'll show up. Surely there are no thieves here."

Zeke looked at the two girls with raised eyebrows. The twins knew they couldn't tell Aunt Bee everything that was going on because she'd tell them not to get involved. But they were sure one of their guests *was* a thief. And if they didn't stop that person, the treasure would be stolen, too.

Jen stepped forward and wiped a smudge of bright red oil paint from Aunt Bee's cheek. "I'm sure the photo will turn up," Jen said, agreeing with her aunt. "I'm starving. Let's eat!"

Aunt Bee didn't say another word about the photograph of Catherine Markham as they helped her lay out the ingredients for a sandwich buffet. Karen also helped, even though Jen and Zeke told her she didn't have to. She was supposed to be on vacation.

"If I sit around, I'll just worry," Karen reasoned, sticking a knife in the mustard.

Just as they were getting ready to eat, Detective Wilson drove up and let himself inside. "What good timing," he joked.

Jen and Zeke grinned. He always had good timing when it came to eating Aunt Bee's food. Even with the electricity off, she made fantastic meals, and Detective Wilson knew it.

Jen thought the retired detective had a crush on Aunt Bee. He was always stopping by to help with repairs around the B&B. One of her fresh-from-the-oven muffins or a slice of blueberry pie was always the perfect reward once the repair was finished.

When all the guests were sitting down to their over-stuffed sandwiches of ham, turkey, or roast beef, Aunt Bee called for everyone's attention. She introduced Detective Wilson, explaining that he would fill their sinks with water so that they could wash up after lunch.

Jen shivered. Washing up in freezing-cold water didn't sound that great. She'd rather wait till the electricity came back on. After all, it was not usually out for more than two days.

"It has been brought to my attention," Aunt Bee continued, "that a photograph from the museum is missing. We do have a mischievous ghost living here who probably moved it as a joke, so if any of you find it, would you please return it?"

After they finished eating, Aunt Bee agreed to give Professor Snyder and Jaspar a "quick and wet" tour of the town.

"I'll just stay here and knit," Mrs. Snyder said when her husband asked if she'd like to join them.

"What are you going to do?" Karen asked her mom.

Mrs. Mills yawned and stretched. "Oooh, I think I'll take a nap. It's perfect napping weather."

After the dining room emptied out, Jen and Zeke cleared the table and prepared to wash the dishes.

"I guess I'll go exploring," Karen said when the twins insisted that she shouldn't help them. "Come find me when you're done."

Zeke nodded. "Don't forget a flashlight," he called after her, knowing she would need it if the storm made the sky any darker.

She held one up, switched it on, and headed for the foyer.

Jen and Zeke hurried through the kitchen chores. They knew they would have to clean the guests' rooms later, but they were hoping that if they finished quickly in the kitchen, they'd have some time for treasure hunting.

As they finished the dishes, Detective Wilson picked up an empty bucket. "I'm going to start filling up everyone's sinks," the retired detective told the twins.

"Do you want us to get our raincoats and help you carry water in from the well?" Zeke asked.

Detective Wilson shook his head. "No, no, I can handle this job myself."

"But—" Zeke tried to interrupt.

Detective Wilson winked. "The more I do, the bigger my payment."

"You mean the bigger the slice of pie you get," Jen said, laughing.

"You've got me pretty well figured out," Detective

Wilson chuckled. He headed outside with the empty bucket and the twins took off before he could change his mind.

"We should find Karen," Zeke said as they were walking into the foyer. "Maybe she found another clue."

Jen agreed and they combed the first floor looking for their friend.

They couldn't find her anywhere downstairs, so they headed up the front staircase. Zeke frowned. "I get the feeling something's not right."

"Do you think she's investigating the tunnels?" asked Jen.

"Maybe," Zeke replied. "But I don't think she'd go without us, now that we're all working together."

Upstairs, they softly called Karen's name.

Zeke stopped. "Did you hear that?"

"Karen?" Jen repeated.

A muffled thump came from somewhere around the corner. The twins tiptoed forward. They peeked down the side hall. Nothing.

"Karen?" Jen called again.

The thump sounded louder.

"It's coming from the hall linen closet," Zeke said, pointing to the closed door.

"Help me!" The distant voice coming from the closet was Karen's.

Mystery and Intrigue

Jen raced forward, hastily turning the old-fashioned key that still stuck out of the lock, and opened the door.

Karen fell out of the linen closet. "I thought you'd never find me," she gasped. Her face was as pale as one of the extra sheets they kept in the closet.

"What happened?"

"I don't really know. I was just looking around up here when I heard a door open somewhere behind me. But before I could turn around, someone shoved me into the closet and locked the door! I was squeezed in there so tight with all the sheets, I felt like a mummy."

"How long were you in there?" Jen asked.

"I don't know. It was probably only a few minutes. Did you pass anyone in the hall?"

Jen shook her head.

Zeke flashed a light on his watch. "We'd better

get to the cleaning. Aunt Bee will be home soon and she'll expect us to have the rooms done."

"I'm coming with you this time," Karen said. "No way am I going to be locked up again. I could have suffocated in there."

The twins retrieved the cleaning supplies from the kitchen and started downstairs with the Snyders' room, the Violet Valley, since they knew the professor was in town and Mrs. Snyder was knitting in the parlor.

"Yuck!" Jen exclaimed. "Look at those disgusting socks. And I thought *your* socks were dirty," she said to her brother.

"Very funny," Zeke said. He liked to take off his shoes and wear socks around the house so his feet wouldn't get cold, which made them dirtier than usual. But these socks looked as if the professor had worn them *outside* without shoes on.

"I'll just sweep them into a corner," Jen said, making a face. "No way am I touching them."

Other than the socks, the Snyders' room was fairly neat. The Professor had three tall stacks of books piled on the dresser and the small bedside table, but at least they weren't thrown all over the room.

"Look at this," Zeke said suddenly. He pointed to one of the books in the highest stack.

Jen walked over with the broom in her hands and tipped her head sideways. "*A Villager's Thoughts on a Small Town.* Hey, that's the book we looked at in the library!"

Zeke carefully examined the binding. "The same book, but not the same copy. This book must belong to the professor because it doesn't have a library label on it."

"Well, he *is* writing a book on Maine," Karen reasoned. "All these other books of his are about small towns in Maine, too."

Jen returned to sweeping. The broom bristles hit something under the bed. Gingerly, she moved the broom so that she could drag the object out of the shadows. In the dim light, she wasn't sure she was seeing the object correctly. She bent down for a closer look.

"You guys!" she exclaimed, picking up the framed photograph. "It's Catherine Markham!"

"How did it get in here?" Zeke demanded.

"I don't know. The Snyders must have taken it," Jen said, gripping the photo in one hand and the broom in the other.

"There's no way to tell who the real thief is without asking them," Zeke said.

"But then they'll know we're up to something," Karen said, panic in her voice. "And they might say something to my mom."

Jen nodded in agreement. "We can't let anyone know about this. Let's just leave it here and see what happens."

No one else could think of anything better to do with the photo, so they agreed. Jen gently slipped it back under the bed.

Next they moved upstairs to the Sunflower Studio. They tapped softly on the door. If Mrs. Mills was asleep already, they didn't want to wake her. When there was no answer, Karen silently opened the door and peeked in.

"She's not here!" Karen exclaimed. She opened

the door a little wider.

"Maybe she couldn't sleep," Jen suggested.

Karen shrugged. "Maybe. But anyway, our room is already neat, thanks to whoever messed it up before."

"Still," Jen said, heading for the bathroom with a bucket and sponge, "we'd better clean. It'll only take a sec."

When they were done, they trudged through the hall to the Rose Room. When they knocked on Esther's door, she called, "Just a minute." She finally opened the door, her head wrapped up in a towel turban. "I was just washing my hair."

"In freezing-cold water?" Jen asked.

"That's right," Esther said. "It was so cold it gave me quite a headache. But at least I have clean hair now."

Jen shivered, imagining the frigid water on her scalp. She'd rather go with dirty hair for an extra day than freeze her brain like that.

"You kids must love living here," Esther said cheerily.

"It's pretty cool," Zeke admitted.

"Imagine having a treasure hidden right here."

Jen and Zeke looked at each other.

"Sure," Jen said. "But we don't know if there really is a treasure. It's probably just a rumor."

"But what if it's true?" Esther went on. "You could

have a real treasure hunt. So much mystery and intrigue!"

The entire time they were in her room, Esther talked and asked questions about life at the B&B, but every other question seemed to refer to the hidden treasure.

After a while, Jen stopped answering, letting Zeke do all the talking. She was afraid she'd let something slip out about the tunnels or the clues.

She breathed a sigh of relief when they finished cleaning and were able to leave. "Esther sure is nosy," she said under her breath.

"Not only that," Zeke said urgently, "but did you see the miniature tape recorder she had on her dresser?"

Jen and Karen shook their heads.

"It was hidden behind the clock. And it was *on* the whole time. She was recording our conversation!"

As they tried to figure out why she was recording what they said, they headed for Jaspar's room. He was still in town, so they quickly swept and dusted, eager to get back to their treasure hunt.

Karen pushed a couple of dresser drawers to close them. "Hey, this drawer is stuck," she said.

Zeke tried to push it in. "That's weird. Something must be jammed in it."

Jen and Karen watched as Zeke pulled the drawer

open before he tried to close it again.

"Look!" Jen exclaimed as something in the drawer caught her eye. "There's a book wedged in there crooked. Look at what it is!"

The three of them stared in amazement at the exact book they had looked at in the library that morning. And this time it wasn't a copy of the book, it was the *same* book. A Mystic Public Library label glowed up at them.

"So he was the one following us," Jen breathed. "He must be trying to find the treasure."

Karen clutched Jen's arm. "Do you think he locked me in the closet?"

"Impossible," Zeke said. "Remember, he's in town with Aunt Bee and Professor Snyder."

"Does that mean there's more than one person after the treasure?" Karen asked.

"Everyone heard about it from your mother," Jen pointed out. "For all we know, *everyone* is hunting for it!"

They headed downstairs to dust the parlor before they put away the cleaning supplies. Mrs. Snyder and Esther were talking.

Zeke nudged Jen and whispered. "Look at Esther. Notice anything strange?"

Jen stared. "Her hair is dry! How could it be dry if she just washed it? There's no electricity for a blow-dryer."

"Exactly."

Suddenly Mrs. Snyder started sneezing and coughing. Zeke pricked up his ears. He could have sworn he heard something, but now all he could hear was Mrs. Snyder blowing her nose. But when the woman took a breath between blows, an eerie wailing filled the room.

12

Trapped

The spooky noise sent shivers down to Jen's toes.

Esther's face suddenly grew pale. "The ghost!" she cried out.

Mrs. Snyder looked worried. But before she could comment, she erupted into another sneezing attack. She dug through her handbag for more tissues, mumbling that she didn't know her husband had returned from town.

"Come on," Zeke said, leaving the parlor. When they were out of earshot he turned to the girls. "That's not a ghost. The sound is coming from the tunnels."

They hurried to the pantry. The secret door was open just a crack, and the strange wailing sound was actually wind whistling through the narrow slit. Zeke opened the door a bit wider and the sound stopped.

Jen grabbed a flashlight and started down the

stairs. "Someone's down there. Let's go!"

"Wait," Zeke called, but Jen kept going. She knew that the only way they'd solve this mystery was to find out who else knew about these tunnels. And the only way to do that was to catch the person right now.

Jen turned on her flashlight and thumped down the stairs, following what she thought were footsteps ahead of her. Zeke and Karen raced after her, but Jen's years on the soccer team had given her extra quickness on her feet. At the foot of the stairs she stopped and held her breath, listening. She waited for Zeke and Karen to catch up.

"I lost him," she said with regret.

Zeke looked around in the dim light. "Hey, what's that?" he said, pointing off to the right into a little nook Jen hadn't noticed before. In the shadowed light it looked like a crouching animal.

They inched forward. Jen jabbed at it with the tip of her shoe, but nothing sprang up at her or bit off her foot. She leaned closer. "It's just dusty clothes," she said finally, "and a pair of boots."

"Why are they down here?"

"Maybe so whoever is hunting for the treasure won't get their regular clothes and shoes dirty. If that person always has clean clothes and shoes, we might never guess he or she has been down here."

"Their feet sure would get dirty on their way to the boots, though," Karen commented. "Just think—"

A creak of wood sounded from the tunnel leading up to the left.

Jen motioned up the set of stairs. "Someone went that way," she whispered. "Where does that tunnel lead?" she asked Karen.

"It goes up to another secret door in one of the guest rooms."

They made their way stealthily up the steps and then down a long tunnel. At the end, the passage turned sharply, revealing another set of stairs. But by the time they got to the top, the tunnel was empty. Whoever it was had exited through a secret door into the Daffodil Den, which was empty this week, and disappeared.

"The only person it could have been," Zeke said when he caught his breath, "was Mrs. Mills." He looked at Karen apologetically.

"It couldn't have been my mother," Karen insisted quickly. "She doesn't care about treasure. Besides, she thinks it's all a big story anyway."

"Maybe we should just see if she's in your room," Zeke suggested.

They trooped to the door of the Sunflower Studio and rapped on it politely. No one answered. They were about to turn and leave when the door opened.

"Hi, kids," Mrs. Mills said. "I thought I heard something. Were you knocking on my door?"

"Yeah," Karen said quickly. "I was looking for you a little while ago. Where were you, Mom?"

Mrs. Mills held up a paperback book. "I was borrowing this from the parlor."

"We didn't see you down there," Zeke said.

"You must have just missed me." Mrs. Mills retreated into her room and flopped back onto the bed. "When I couldn't nap, I decided I'd read. Was there something you wanted, honey?"

Jen heard several male voices coming from downstairs. Aunt Bee, Jaspar, and the Professor had returned. She turned to Karen. "We'll see you later. Try to find out what's going on," she added in a whisper.

Karen nodded and closed the door between them.

On the way downstairs, Jen stopped Zeke on the middle step. "Did you notice?"

Zeke nodded glumly. "How could I miss it? Mrs. Mills's shoes were dusty and smudged just like ours. She must have been in the tunnels."

"Not only that," Jen added, "she was missing a button on her sweater. A sparkly round button that matched the one we found in the tunnel!"

They started down the stairs again. "That means

Mrs. Mills is definitely after the treasure. But does Karen know?"

"Maybe, maybe not. Let's just keep an eye on her. I like Karen and I don't want to hurt her feelings by accusing her mother of lying to us."

By dinnertime the storm was starting to clear. Electricity still hadn't been restored to the B&B, but Aunt Bee guessed it was only a matter of hours before they'd have power again. The guests all cheered.

"Though I do love eating by candlelight," Esther gushed.

"I prefer electricity," Jaspar grumbled. But he couldn't keep a sour face for long and grinned.

"Why are you so happy?" Professor Snyder asked.

"Well, I really shouldn't tell you," Jaspar admitted. "My next live television special has been approved."

"What is it?" Jen asked.

"I really can't tell you." He winked. "It's a big secret."

Jen's stomach squeezed uncomfortably. *Could his special have anything to do with the hidden treasure?* She glanced at Zeke and then Karen. They were obviously all thinking the same thing.

The three of them soon excused themselves, promising Aunt Bee they would do the dishes later. They headed into the foyer where no one could hear them.

"Jaspar must be after the treasure," Karen wailed. "He's going to ruin everything. I just know Catherine Markham would hate her treasure to be on TV."

"Then there's only one thing to do," Jen said, agreeing with Karen. "We have to find it first!"

"But we haven't figured out the last clue," Zeke said.

"We don't have time for that now," Jen insisted. "The most obvious place for the treasure to be hidden is in the tunnels. We'll just have to dig around till we find it. As soon as everyone goes to bed, we have to go down there."

It wasn't until eleven that Zeke felt confident that everyone had settled down for the night. The twins met Karen in the parlor just as the clock was striking eleven-fifteen.

"Ready?" Zeke whispered.

"Did you bring your flashlight?" Jen asked her brother. The tunnels were always pitch-black, but going down there late at night was somehow spookier.

"I couldn't find it."

"Me neither."

"Someone doesn't want us snooping around!"

"We'll have to use a lantern," Jen said, taking the

one that sat on the foyer counter. She lit it carefully. The light wavered as they made their way through the silent B&B to the secret door in the parlor.

Taking a deep breath, Jen said, "I'll go first since I'm holding the light." No one argued with her.

It seemed to take forever to descend the thirty steps. At last they reached the rocky floor of the tunnel. They were huddled together and the feeble light from the lantern didn't reach very far.

"See anything yet?" Karen whispered.

"The clothes are missing," Jen hissed.

They all looked at the shallow alcove where they had last seen the pile of clothes and the boots. The space was bare.

"Not even a single clue," Zeke said, frowning. "Let's go look in that storage room you mentioned. Maybe you missed something in there."

Keeping so close together made it hard to walk, but the three of them continued down the tunnel. At the three-way split, they turned off to the left. The path sloped down a bit, and before long they found themselves in a room carved out of the rock. It seemed to be as large as the parlor. As Karen had described, old, empty bookshelves leaned against the walls.

Jen opened her mouth to say something, but Zeke

held up his hand for quiet. An odd scraping sound filled the silence.

Jen felt like her ears were going to explode, she was listening so hard, but the sound had stopped.

Zeke motioned for them to walk quietly back to the main tunnel. Still holding the lantern, Jen knew she'd have to go first. Dread weighed down her feet. Each step was a chore. All she wanted to do was hide in a corner. *Are we crazy to be down here in the middle of the night?* But even as this thought ran through her head, she put one foot in front of the other.

The light in the lantern flickered in a sudden breeze. Jen moved her hand up to block the light wind. Too late! The light blew out, leaving them in complete darkness.

13

The Key

Karen let out a little squeak, but it sounded more like a rusty hinge than anything human.

Someone tugged on Jen's arm and she nearly dropped the dark lantern.

"Shhhhh," Zeke hissed.

Jen bit her tongue to keep from shouting. She felt totally lost. Which way was out? Then she heard the scraping sound again. Or was it a dragging sound?

Zeke felt Karen tense beside him. Suddenly, she erupted into a fit of sneezing. The dust!

The odd sound stopped. Then, a huge shape pushed past them. The kids were scattered in the narrow tunnel like bowling pins. Whoever it was held a dim flashlight, and Jen caught a glimpse of dusty clothes and heavy boots.

"Hey!" Zeke shouted, but the soft sound of

running feet didn't stop. A few seconds later there was complete silence—and total darkness again.

"Is everyone okay?" he whispered, worried that the intruder might still be lurking in the tunnels.

"I'm okay," Jen said. Her voice sounded a bit shaky.

"Me, too," Karen said from off to the left. "Who was that?"

Jen said, "Whoever he was—"

"Or she," Zeke interrupted.

"—has some explaining to do. I nearly cracked my skull open on the wall."

"I didn't hear the lantern break."

Jen grinned in the darkness. "I might have broken my head, but I saved the lamp."

"Let's get out of here," Karen said.

"Let's go this way," Zeke said. "This is the way the intruder went, so it must be the way out."

In the inky blackness, Jen grabbed a piece of Zeke's shirt with one hand. Behind her, Karen did the same to her shirt. Attached like a train, the three of them slowly chugged their way down the passage. At last they rounded a bend and Zeke nearly tripped over the first step up. Even though he knew they were finally close to getting out of the tunnels, his heart didn't stop hammering until they reached the top of the stairs.

Breathing a huge sigh of relief, they stepped out of

the passage and closed the secret door behind them. Shafts of light from the full moon were streaming into the parlor, giving them enough light to see. They seemed like spotlights to Jen after the complete blackness of the tunnels.

"Let's go up to my room to talk," Zeke whispered.

They made their way silently to the still-dark lighthouse tower and climbed the circular stairs up to Zeke's room.

"Cool," Karen said, examining his room by moonlight. She moved to a window. "Wow, great view."

Jen and Zeke crowded behind her to look out. "There's an even better view from the observation platform on the top," Zeke said. "But the lighthouse lamp is so bright that it's hard to get a good view at night. During the day the view is great."

"We could go see the view now," Jen commented. "The lighthouse is dark because we still don't have electricity."

Zeke snapped his fingers. "That's it!"

"What's it?" Karen asked, turning away from the window.

Zeke didn't answer. All he said was, "Come on!"

He dashed for the stairs that led up to the platform. The metal circular stairs rang with each hurried footstep, echoing all the way down the stairwell. They burst through the door onto the observation deck.

The view was breathtaking. The moon had sneaked out from behind a storm cloud and scattered moonlight gleamed like quicksilver on the Atlantic Ocean. Although the storm had started to clear, the water was still rough, and it whipped and crashed on the rocks far below them. For a long moment, no one spoke.

Finally Zeke said, "Okay, what do you see?"

"The ocean," Karen said, sounding doubtful. "But so what?"

Zeke huffed with impatience. "What else do you see?"

"The rocks below, the roof of the house," Jen answered.

"The bay," Karen added. "Clouds."

Jen put her hand on Karen's arm to stop her. She peered through the night. Sure enough, there was the bay. Beyond that she could just make out—"The distant shore!" she exclaimed.

"Exactly!" exclaimed Zeke.

"When the lighthouse is dark," Karen recited from memory, "the distant shore is the mark."

"The clue," Jen said. "It must lead up here."

"Catherine Markham must have hidden a clue up here that can only be found when the lighthouse is dark," said Zeke. "When the light is on, it is too bright up here to see the distant shore."

"But they didn't have electricity back then," Karen said, sounding confused. "Professor Snyder said that the lighthouse keeper filled the oil lamps twice a night to keep the light burning, so why would it ever be dark?"

"Maybe if he got too sick," Jen said. "Then maybe the lighthouse did go dark."

"Let's look along the side of the lighthouse that faces the distant shore," Zeke said, already crouching down to examine the stone wall that circled the platform. The three of them hunted in silence.

Jen leaned over the wall, trying not to notice how far down the rocks were. With her heart in her throat, she was about to give up her search when a glimmer of something caught her eye. But when she looked again, the glimmer was gone. Figuring it must have been a figment of her imagination, she was about to turn away when the moon broke through a hazy cloud. The shimmering globe illuminated everything so brightly that the night suddenly seemed to be day.

Jen took one more look over the edge of the wall. Yes! There was something shiny between two stone blocks that seemed to pick up the light of the moon and glow with a blue hue. It was just within reach. She pulled. It came loose in her fingers. With a cry of dismay, Jen felt it drop free and plunge out of sight.

Zeke and Karen gathered on either side of her. "What happened?"

Karen gulped and moved away from the wall. "That is way scary," she said.

"I saw something shine in the moonlight. But when I dug it out, it fell out of my hand. I think I lost the clue!" She leaned over the wall and poked her fingers in the hole left by the missing rock. "Wait a minute. I didn't," she said triumphantly. "I found the clue!" She

stood back, clutching something in her hand. She gave it to Karen. "It's your treasure hunt, so you look at it."

Karen carefully unfolded the old piece of paper. "It's oil paper," she said. "It's what they used to use to keep things dry before they had plastic wrap and waxed paper. But now it's old and crumbly."

The paper fell away to reveal another folded paper. When Karen carefully unfolded that one, they were amazed to see an old-fashioned key.

"That looks like the old key in the upstairs linen closet," Jen said. "What's it for?"

Karen shook her head. "Listen to this." She began reading. "*I, Jacob Markham*—that was Catherine's father," she added, "*do hereby swear to keep the light-house lamp burning from this day forth until the day I die.*"

"I thought that was his job," Jen interrupted.

"*No more will I purposely let the lamp go out so that ships will be lost and crash upon the shore.*"

The three of them gasped.

"*No more will I purposely lead ships onto the rocks with a lantern burning too far inland. No more will I steal from the wreckage nor collect the wealth the waves leave at my cruel hand. I will repent of the murders I have caused, now and forevermore.*"

14

Missing Clues

"I can't believe it," Jen finally breathed. "There wasn't a Ghost of the Dark Lighthouse. It was the keeper himself who let the lighthouse go dark!"

The three of them peeked over the wall, imagining the ships smashing onto the rocks far below. They hadn't crashed accidentally, but because Catherine's father had purposely led them onto the rocks so he could steal from the wrecked ships.

"How awful," Karen said.

"Catherine must have figured out what her father was doing and made him promise to stop," Zeke said. "And if he did it again, she'd use this confession against him."

Karen gulped. "I wonder what happened to her. Her diary ends the very same day this letter was written," she noted.

"What's the key for?" Jen asked.

"I don't know," Karen said, examining the key more closely. She handed it to Jen, then turned the letter over. "Hey, there's more." She turned the paper to catch the moonlight. "I can hardly read it. It seems to have some water damage or something. *I have hidden the treasures I stole . . .*"

"Where?" Jen exclaimed.

"It's all smudged. The only thing I can read is at the end where it says, *to use for a worthy cause.*"

"So there really *is* a treasure hidden somewhere," Zeke said. "That must be what the key is for."

"Now we just have to find it," Jen said.

"Unless someone else already has," Zeke said darkly. "Maybe that's the noise we heard in the tunnel tonight—someone dragging a treasure chest."

"And whoever it was didn't want to get caught," Karen said, rubbing her elbow where it had banged against the tunnel wall.

"But the thief won't have the key to open the treasure chest," Jen pointed out hopefully. "We just have to find where it's hidden and unlock it."

Jen handed the key back to Karen, who shivered. "But not tonight," Karen said. "I'm freezing, and my mom's going to worry about me if she notices I'm not in our room. We'll have to figure this out tomorrow morning. The treasure's safe as long as we have the key."

The three retraced their steps down the dark stairwell. Jen lit a lantern and walked Karen to her room so that she wouldn't bump into any of the furniture, then she returned to Zeke's room. She knew neither one of them would get any sleep until they talked about the mystery of the dark lighthouse.

Sure enough, Zeke was waiting for her. He'd lit a candle and already had sheets of paper in front of him. When she walked in with the lantern, he blew out the candle.

"It's time to fill out suspect sheets," he said. "It's the only way we'll figure out who else is searching for the treasure."

"All the guests look guilty to me. Even Mrs. Snyder, if you think about it."

Zeke raised his eyebrows. "How could she be guilty? All she does is sit in the parlor all day and sneeze."

"Exactly," Jen exclaimed. "Doesn't that seem a bit strange to you? And after all, the photograph *was* under her bed."

Zeke pondered that a second. "You're right," he said slowly. "But that doesn't make her guilty of pushing us over in the tunnels or leaving footprints in there."

Jen sighed. "True. But it must mean something."

Zeke picked up his pen. "Let's write down what we know."

Mystic Lighthouse

Suspect Sheet

Name: Esther Barr

Motive: Wants the treasure?

Clues: WHY IS SHE AVOIDING JASPAR?

Who was she talking to about the treasure? What did she mean when she said "do anything to get that treasure . . . whatever necessary to find it"?

SHE ASKED A LOT OF QUESTIONS ABOUT THE TREASURE, AND SHE IS TAPE RECORDING THE INFORMATION.

Why was she nosing around the B&B? She was looking for something on the check-in counter but said she was just looking for a pen, which was in plain view.

She couldn't have opened the secret passage door when we heard it moaning— she was in the parlor with Mrs. Snyder.

Why did she say she'd just washed her hair when she really hadn't? (Her hair was dry, but there was no electricity for a hair dryer!)

Mystic Lighthouse

Suspect Sheet

Name: JASPAR WESTCOMBE

Motive: *Professional investigative reporter and treasure hunter*

Clues: HE KNOWS A LOT ABOUT TREASURE AND COULD HAVE KNOWN ABOUT THE LIGHTHOUSE TREASURE BEFORE HE CAME.

WHO IS HE TALKING TO ON THE PHONE ALL THE TIME?

Why is he trying to talk to Esther, who keeps trying to avoid him?

ARE THOSE HIS FOOTPRINTS IN THE SECRET PASSAGEWAYS?

Why did he follow us to the library?

HAS BOOK IN ROOM ABOUT THE TREASURE AND SECRET PASSAGES THAT HE GOT FROM THE LIBRARY.

HE HAS A NEW SHOW HE'S EXCITED ABOUT—COULD IT BE THE LIGHTHOUSE TREASURE?

Mystic Lighthouse

Suspect Sheet

Name: Professor Snyder

Motive: Wants to discover a part of history and wants the treasure

Clues: He admits he knows a lot about Mystic. He could have known about the treasure before he got here, also could know about the secret doors.

His suitcase was heavy—could he have been hiding tools in it?

Are those his footprints in the secret passage?

The Christmas photo was in his room.

But he wasn't at the B&B when the secret passage was opened to make that moaning sound.

Mystic Lighthouse

Suspect Sheet

Name: Mrs. Snyder

Motive: Wants the treasure for her husband?

Clues: KNOWS A LOT ABOUT MYSTIC THROUGH HER HUSBAND?

If she's really hard of hearing, why doesn't she wear a hearing aid? And why can she hear some things some of the time? Is she faking it?

She had a treasure-hunting book in her purse.

WHY WAS SHE SO INTERESTED WHEN WE WERE IN THE BATHROOM?

The Christmas photo was in her room.

She was in the parlor when the passage door was opened so she couldn't have done it.

Mystic Lighthouse

Suspect Sheet

Name: Lenore Mills

Motive: Wants the treasure?

Clues: SAYS THE TREASURE IS JUST A
SILLY STORY, BUT MAYBE THAT'S JUST
TO THROW OTHERS OFF THE TRACK.

PROBABLY KNOWS A LOT OF
INFORMATION FROM HEARING IT FROM
KAREN OVER THE YEARS.

Karen says she definitely knows about
the secret passages because Karen
told her all about them.

Her button was in the secret passage.
Were her footprints in the tunnels?

SUPPOSEDLY TAKING A NAP, BUT WE
COULDN'T FIND HER ANYWHERE.

Acted embarrassed when questioned
about where she was when the secret
passage door was opened.

SHE HAD DIRTY SHOES!

When they finished, Jen reread their notes out loud. She sighed with disgust and threw the papers on the desk. "That was about zero help."

"We must be missing something," Zeke said thoughtfully. "Did we forget to write down a clue?"

Jen shook her head. "I don't think so. We'll just have to figure it out tomorrow. . . . I just hope we're not too late."

Note to Reader

Have you figured out who else is on the hunt for the treasure? Jen and Zeke have made pretty good notes on the suspects, but they did miss a few very important clues. Without those clues, it's almost impossible to figure out who the mysterious treasure hunter is.

Have you come to a conclusion? Take your time. Carefully review the suspect sheets. Fill in any details Jen and Zeke missed. When you think you have a solution, read the last chapter to find out if Jen and Zeke can put all the pieces together to solve *The Mystery of the Dark Lighthouse*.

Good luck!

Solution

Another Mystery
Solved!

Zeke slept fitfully that night. He dreamed about large, ornate keys and old-fashioned sailing ships. When it was finally time to get up, he was thrilled to see that the rest of the clouds had disappeared and the sun was shining brightly. The storm was over!

He flicked his light switch, but the power was still off. He knew it'd be back on shortly. He threw on his clothes and banged on Jen's door on his way down the stairs. She came out of her room looking bleary-eyed. Slinky darted down the stairs.

"I had the worst dreams last night," she admitted when Zeke said she looked tired. "Catherine kept leading me into the tunnels and then leaving me all alone in the dark. It was so spooky."

"It was probably just her ghost telling you to hurry up and find the treasure," Zeke teased.

Before Jen could respond, they were in the dining room and Karen was hurrying over to them. "Guess what," she whispered. "The key is gone!"

"What?" Jen exclaimed.

"Shhhh."

"Someone stole the key out of your room last night?" Zeke asked.

"No, no," Karen said soothingly. "I still have the treasure chest key. I mean the one in the hall closet that I was locked in. Remember how you said it looked like the one we found?" she reminded Jen.

The twins nodded.

"Well, on my way down here this morning, I wanted to compare them, but the key is missing from the closet door. I'll bet the thief stole the key to try it in the treasure chest!"

"That means we don't have much time," Zeke said urgently. "Sometimes those old locks will open even if the key isn't the exact one made for the lock. We have to find that treasure before whoever it is tries the key."

"That means we have to go into the tunnels now," Jen said, glancing around to make sure no one was eavesdropping.

"Let's go," Karen said. "I took my mom's flashlight and I have the key. We have to hurry."

Slipping quietly and, they hoped, unnoticed into the kitchen, the three of them hurried to the secret door in the pantry. Jen took a deep breath before following the other two into the murky darkness. Even with the flashlight, it seemed spooky in the tunnels.

At the bottom of the stairs, Zeke stopped them. "I thought I heard something."

They all froze and listened.

"I don't hear anything," Jen finally whispered.

Zeke shrugged doubtfully. "Okay, let's go, but be as quiet as you can."

At the second fork in the path, they decided to check the storage room. The room was empty. Then they retraced their steps and stood at the fork again.

"Look!" Zeke crouched down and examined the floor. "See these drag marks?"

Jen leaned over and peered at the ground. "It looks like someone was dragging a heavy chest."

"I bet that's what we heard yesterday," Karen said. "The marks lead down there." She pointed.

No one said anything for a second. The drag marks led straight to the set of stairs that led even deeper underground.

"Where does this path lead?" Jen whispered.

"I don't know," Karen admitted. "Remember, I was too chicken to check it out."

Zeke stood up. "We're about to find out. Come on."

Jen felt as if she were being buried alive as she stepped down and down and down. The stairs were never-ending. The air got colder and there was definitely a strong breeze. They thought that they must have been getting closer to the ocean, because the sound of crashing waves was getting louder and louder.

After what seemed like an hour, they reached the bottom of the stairs.

"I think I know where we are." Zeke had to raise his voice to be heard over the sound of the waves. "These are the caves at the bottom of the cliffs. When the tide is in, like now, the caves are hidden, but at low tide you can get into them from the shore."

"This must have been how Catherine's father hid all the treasure from the wrecked ships," Jen said. "He dragged it from the sea into these caves and then carried it up through the secret tunnels."

Karen flashed the light back and forth. "Let's look around."

Zeke stopped and cocked his head.

"What is it?" Jen asked.

"I keep thinking I hear something."

"The ocean," Jen said.

Zeke shrugged. "Must be."

The underground caves were divided into three

parts. One part was a huge cavern where the kids couldn't see the ceiling. Sprouting off that cave there was a low tunnel that led to a smaller cave filled with glittering crystals.

"Are these diamonds?" Jen breathed in awe.

"No," Zeke said. "Probably just salt crystals."

Another low tunnel led down to the opening of the cave. But because the tide was high, the passage soon became flooded.

"We'd better not go this way," Zeke said. "We'll have to come back when the tide is out and the ocean is calm. It's still churned up from the storm."

Jen quickly agreed, not eager to get her feet sopping wet. They all turned around and inspected the third section of the cave, which was on the far wall of the huge cavern. It was honeycombed with small, shallow caves that had been dug out of the wall. Each cave was big enough to fit two or three seated people. Jen counted at least ten of these strange indentations in the wall.

"Look!" Karen shouted. She shone her light on the far left hole.

Jen's heart pounded louder than the waves with excitement as the three of them rushed over to a treasure chest partly hidden in one of the small caverns. Someone had tried to tuck the chest as far back as possible, but it was too big and bulky to hide completely.

They crouched down in front of it. With shaking fingers, Karen withdrew the old key from her pocket.

"Stop right there!" someone shouted behind them.

The three of them whirled around.

"You!" Zeke exclaimed.

Professor Snyder shrugged. "I knew you kids would find the treasure sooner or later. I'm glad that you did. Now give me the key." He held out his hand.

A flicker of light behind the professor caught Jen's eye. She grabbed the key from Karen as the Professor stepped forward.

"No," Jen cried. "You can't have it."

The professor took a menacing step toward her. "Give it to me now. I don't have time for this."

There was a sudden clatter from the tunnel. Professor Snyder whipped around to see what the noise was.

Mrs. Mills stepped forward. "The key belongs to my daughter and her friends," Mrs. Mills said sharply. "I suggest you stay right there," she threatened when the professor looked as if he might lunge at her. "The police are right behind me." She dug a length of rope from her back pocket and tossed it to Zeke. "Tie him up."

Zeke grinned. This weekend wasn't turning out so badly after all! As he moved forward with the rope in his hands, Aunt Bee and Detective Wilson stumbled into the stone cavern.

"What's going on?" Aunt Bee exclaimed.

Detective Wilson immediately hurried over to help Zeke. It took only five minutes to explain what had happened.

Grinning, Jen finally said, "Let's get this treasure up to the B&B. I'm dying to see what's inside."

It took quite a bit of lugging and hauling to heave the chest up all the stairs and through the tunnels into the pantry. They finally pulled it into the dining room. The other guests heard the commotion and gathered around.

"The treasure!" Esther exclaimed. "How absolutely, positively perfect!"

"Is that really it?" Jaspar asked, taking a closer look at the old chest.

"We think so," Zeke said.

Mrs. Snyder came into the room at that moment and cried out in dismay. "I knew this wouldn't work. I told you not to sneak around like that," she said to her husband.

Professor Snyder bowed his head sheepishly. "I only wanted it for research, but the more I hunted for it, the more gold and jewels I imagined in the chest. I knew that Jacob Markham had wrecked ships and plundered them. I started to get as greedy as he was. I'm sorry. I'm sorry I sneaked around and stole the photograph. I guess I was possessed by treasure fever. I even searched your room," he added, glancing at Karen and her mother.

Mrs. Snyder shook her head. "I guess I might as well admit to everyone that I'm not really hard of hearing. I'm sorry I lied to you all."

"I knew it," Zeke said. "You were the lookout for the professor."

Mrs. Snyder nodded. "That's right. Whenever he got too loud digging in the tunnels, I started coughing and sneezing to warn him. I pretended to be hard of hearing because I knew if you heard the noises and noticed I started coughing every time, eventually you would put two and two together."

Jen remembered the time she'd heard a strange noise that stopped after Mrs. Snyder's sneezing attack. It all made sense now. She turned to the professor again. "And you kept some clothes and boots in the tunnels to wear while you were digging around, right?"

The professor nodded. "I didn't want my dirty, dusty clothes or shoes to give me away."

"But your socks did," Zeke interjected. "We saw them in your room when we were cleaning. I just didn't figure out why your socks were so dirty until it was too late," he admitted.

"What about you?" Jen asked, turning to Mrs. Mills. "How did you find us in time?"

"Oh, I knew you kids were up to something. Aunt Bee keeps this place really clean, so I couldn't figure out why the three of you had dirty shoes all the time. I finally figured out there really must be tunnels in this place. So I did a little sleuthing of my own and found the secret entrance to the tunnels. In fact, remember that moaning sound you heard?"

The three kids nodded.

"That was because of me. I left the pantry door open a little so I could find my way out. I never dreamed it would create a wind tunnel and cause all that noise. When I heard you coming, I ran away. I didn't want you to think I didn't trust you and was spying on you," she said, looking at Karen.

"But you found the tunnels before we did," Jen said. "Because I picked up your missing button in there the first time Zeke and I were in there."

Mrs. Mills frowned. "I was missing that button long before I found the secret entrance. How strange."

Slinky meowed loudly and rubbed against Jen's leg. Jen laughed and picked up the cat. "You little thief. Slinky must have been playing with the button when she got stuck in the tunnels."

"This morning," Mrs. Mills continued her story, "I saw you three disappear, then I noticed the professor following you. I didn't know exactly what was going on, but I thought I should keep an eye on things. I followed Professor Snyder as he followed you."

"And it's a good thing you brought rope," Jen said, laughing.

Mrs. Mills grinned. "I had it with me to tie down the loose luggage rack on the rental car. It knocked all the way here from the airport and nearly drove me crazy. I was going to tie it down before we headed back to the airport this afternoon."

Aunt Bee shuddered. "I'm so glad I had no idea all of this was going on. I'm old enough as it is."

Zeke hugged his aunt. "You saved the day," he told her. "If you and Detective Wilson hadn't come to the rescue, who knows what might have happened."

"How did you know about the tunnels anyway?" Jen asked.

Aunt Bee looked at her. "I just happened to see Mrs. Mills wander into the kitchen. I followed her, thinking she was looking for something else to eat. When she disappeared into the pantry, I rushed to get Detective Wilson. Luckily he was here early today to help with the roof leak on the third floor. Anyway, we found the secret door in the pantry and followed the sound of talking until we reached you." She put a hand over her heart. "I'm just so glad we arrived in time."

"Me, too," Jen said. Then she flung a hand toward the chest. "Let's open the treasure!" She couldn't stand another second of suspense.

Karen took out the key and inserted it into the lock. Jen and Zeke held their breath as Karen turned the key. Click.

Moving slowly, as though afraid that a ghost would jump out at her, Karen lifted the lid.

Everyone gasped. No wonder the trunk had been so heavy and hard to lug up the stairs. It was full to the brim with golden cups and pieces of jewelry. There were necklaces with pearls the size of marbles, and even a dagger with diamonds and rubies embedded in the hilt.

Karen ignored all the jewels and reached for a pile of leather-bound books. "The rest of Catherine's diaries," she breathed with satisfaction. She started thumbing through them as the rest of the group sifted through the unbelievable treasure.

"There must be over a million dollars' worth of stuff in here," Zeke said.

Deeper in the trunk there wasn't as much gold and jewelry, but there were lengths of fabric with gold thread sewn through them and old-fashioned shoes with pearl buttons that looked like new. There were three silver mirrors that were tarnished nearly black, but Jen could tell from the intricately carved frames and handles that they would be beautiful when polished.

"This is almost as exciting as uncovering the Egyptian tomb," Jaspar commented.

Zeke asked him, "You never had anything to do with hunting for the treasure, did you?"

The TV reporter cleared his throat. "Well, I do admit I was intrigued. I followed you kids to the library without your knowing it."

Jen and Zeke looked at each other and grinned, but didn't interrupt.

"Then I took out the book you'd looked at," Jaspar continued. "But it didn't have much information in it. I was going to search a little more for the treasure, thinking it'd be fun, but then my producer called about my next story and I've been busy working on it ever since."

"Your story had nothing to do with the treasure?" Jen asked.

"Of course not," Jaspar said, looking a bit insulted. "I have to go for *big* stories."

Karen laughed. "We think this *is* a big story."

"I'm afraid it wouldn't bring in the ratings," Jaspar said.

"Why were you trying to talk to Esther all the time?" Jen asked, a little upset that he thought

Mystic, Maine, wasn't big enough to do a story about.

Jaspar glanced at Esther and shrugged. "I'm afraid that's not for me to say. I promised."

Esther sighed and rolled her eyes. "Oh, I may as well tell you, since you feel like family now." In one graceful sweep, she pulled off her straight black hair. Under the wig she had short blond hair.

"Esther Barrimore!" Aunt Bee cried. "The famous mystery author. I love your books. I knew you looked familiar!"

Esther smiled. "Yes, I'm afraid I've been living a bit of a lie. I came here as Esther Barr to get away for a few days. But as soon as I got here I realized this is the perfect setting for my next mystery. I've been taking notes like crazy. I didn't want Jaspar, who has interviewed me a number of times and recognized me right away, to blow my cover. When people find out who I am they want to ask me all sorts of questions, and I never get any work done."

"Do you happen to take notes on a miniature tape recorder?" Zeke asked.

"How did you know that? I thought I had hidden it from everyone."

Zeke grinned. "I saw it running in your room when we were cleaning and you were asking all those questions. And you must have been recording ideas for the mystery when I overheard you talking about the treasure yesterday after breakfast."

Esther patted him on the back. "You are quite the detective, young man. Perhaps I'll have to put you in my next book."

Jen took a turn to add her own clues. "When you said you'd just washed your hair, you really hadn't, had you?"

"No," Esther admitted. "I just put the towel on to cover my real hair when you knocked on my door. The wig wasn't as easy to put on as a towel was. And I have another awful confession to make."

Everyone waited expectantly while Esther took a deep breath. She turned to Karen. "I was the one who locked you in the closet. I was out of my room and I heard you coming. I couldn't let you see me without my wig on, so I pushed you in the closet. You didn't get hurt, did you?"

Karen shook her head.

"I went to put on my wig and then I was going to let you out, but you were already gone when I came back. I am so sorry."

Karen smiled. "It's okay. I was only in there a couple of minutes."

Esther sighed with relief. "And you probably thought I was a real snoop, but I was just trying to get a feeling for the B&B and how it runs and looks."

Jen grinned. "We were wondering when we caught you looking for a pen and they were right there in front of you."

Esther blushed. "It's the curse of a writer to be nosy!"

Professor Snyder coughed. "What's going to happen to me?"

Detective Wilson frowned. "You didn't hurt anyone and you don't have a weapon. But you did steal the photograph and the clue." He turned to Aunt Bee. "Do you want to press any charges?"

Aunt Bee sighed. "No. Treasure and riches certainly do bring out the worst in people. Let him go."

Detective Wilson untied the professor and, with heads bowed in shame, the Snyders left to pack their bags.

"Listen to this," Karen said. She removed a loose sheet of paper from one of the diaries. "Catherine wrote this when she was seventy-six. *'Herein lie my diaries. I have lived a full life with thirteen children, twenty-seven grandchildren, and four great-grandchildren. Over the years, I have used Father's ill-begotten riches to help the poor and needy. I pray that whoever finds this will continue to offer help where it is needed. When you think of my father, Jacob Markham, think not with malice and scorn, but know that he did repent and never again did the lighthouse go dark.'* She signed it and dated it 1966."

No one spoke. Jen tried to imagine the young girl in front of the Christmas tree growing old, giving away money, probably in secret, to those who needed it. She blinked back the tears that filled her eyes. Even though she knew it was impossible, she wished there were some way she could have known Catherine Markham.

"I think the treasure should stay here," Karen said thoughtfully. She turned to Aunt Bee. "Will you make sure the right people get it?"

"Certainly," Aunt Bee said. Zeke could see that his aunt was touched. "Are you sure?"

Karen nodded. "The money should stay in Mystic and be given back to the descendants of the lost sailors."

Aunt Bee nodded. "I agree, and I'm sure I'll find a fair way to distribute the funds, perhaps college scholarships, and new books for the library, and . . ."

Jen laughed, jerking her thumb in her aunt's direction. "She won't have any problem sharing the wealth, that's for sure."

Karen smiled and gently rubbed her hand over the worn leather bindings. "I just want these diaries."

Suddenly, all the lights in the B&B blazed on. The group cheered.

"Treasure and electricity in one day!" Zeke said, laughing.

"Can't get richer than that," Jen added with a smile.

Later that afternoon, Jen and Zeke waved good-bye as all the guests left. As the last car drove off down the long driveway, Jen sighed. "This wasn't such a bad weekend after all."

On the way to her room, Jen stopped to look at the photo of Catherine Markham standing in front of the Christmas tree. She rubbed her eyes, sure she was imagining it. But it seemed to her that Catherine's smile was a lot wider than it had been before.

The Mystery
of Dead Man's Curve

*This book is dedicated to all
of Mrs. Henneberry's students—
past, present, and future*

Contents

Attempted Murder

"They'll be here any minute," Aunt Bee called out as she pulled at her flowing skirt to make sure it was hanging straight. She eyed the foyer to double-check that everything was in place and nervously fussed with the flowers sitting on the front desk.

Jen looked over at her twin brother, Zeke, and they both grinned. Even though the Mystic Lighthouse Bed and Breakfast had been open for two years, Aunt Bee still got nervous before new guests arrived.

"Don't worry," Jen teased, tugging on her aunt's long gray braid. "Zeke and I cleaned all the rooms that will be used, put full toilet paper rolls in the bathrooms, and even washed the windows. Everything is ready."

Bee straightened the registration book on the desk for the third time. "Did you change the sheets?"

Jen gasped. "Oh, no, we forgot the beds!"

Zeke tried to hide his smile. "The beds! How will our guests sleep tonight?"

Aunt Bee scowled as she lunged playfully at her niece and nephew. Jen laughed and expertly ducked out of Aunt Bee's reach, but Zeke wasn't as quick. Their aunt caught him and gave him a big bear hug before letting him go with a giant kiss on the cheek.

Zeke wiped it away with pretended disgust. He always thought it was funny that his aunt got so nervous about guests arriving. After all, she had run the B&B since it opened. With the twins' help, of course. Jen and Zeke had moved in with their aunt Bee and uncle Cliff nine years ago, after their parents died. That was when the twins were just two-year-old toddlers. Their uncle Cliff passed away just before the B&B's grand opening. Aunt Bee was the only family member Jen and Zeke had left. Even though they called her Aunt Bee, she was more like a mother to them. Or a grandmother, actually, because she was really their grandma Estelle's sister.

Slinky, their Maine coon cat, jumped down from a high cabinet and swished her fluffy tail back and forth. With a long meow, she stepped on top of Woofer, their Old English sheepdog. Woofer, asleep as usual, opened one lazy eye, then quickly closed it.

He was used to Slinky walking on him and obviously didn't want to interrupt his nap to shake her off. Aunt Bee and the twins laughed.

"As you know," Aunt Bee said, quickly getting back to business, "the five guests we're having this week are all candidates for the principal's job at Mystic Middle School. So you two had better be on your best behavior."

"Aren't we always?" Jen asked with a mischievous little smile.

"Most of the time," Aunt Bee admitted. "But not always. Besides, don't you want to make a good impression on your new principal?"

"I guess so," Jen agreed.

"Of course," Zeke said.

Aunt Bee smiled at them. "Good. Now let's do one more sweep in here."

Zeke looked at the hardwood floors that already glowed with polish. He supposed it wouldn't hurt to sweep the corners of the foyer. "I'll go get the broom," he offered.

Jen eyed the floor. "It doesn't look dirty to me. I just mopped it yesterday."

Aunt Bee adjusted the curtains. "A little sweeping won't kill you."

Jen groaned. "It might."

"Sometimes I can't believe you and Zeke are twins," Aunt Bee said, laughing. "You look the same, with your dark wavy hair and bright blue eyes, but why is he so neat and you're so not?"

"He's one minute older than me," Jen said with a grin. "That makes him more responsible."

Zeke returned from the kitchen with the broom and dustpan and started to sweep the corners of the room. Jen couldn't see a speck of dust, but Zeke kept sweeping as if there were piles of dirt. He bent over and poked the broom under the cabinet. When he pulled out the broom, a dust ball filled with cat hair came along with it.

"Good job mopping yesterday," Zeke teased his twin, a sparkle lighting up his blue eyes.

Jen shrugged. "Oops." She moved closer to the mess. "Hey, what's that?" Gingerly, she tugged on a string that was snaking out from under the cabinet. When she pulled, her neon-green yo-yo rolled out. "Jeez, this has been missing for weeks!" she exclaimed. "How did it get under there?"

"It's that rascal Slinky," Aunt Bee said from the other side of the foyer where she was plumping the floral cushions on each overstuffed chair. "She'll steal anything she can get her paws on."

Using the Mystic, Maine, T-shirt she was wearing,

Jen rubbed the dust and hair off her yo-yo.

Aunt Bee looked at her with one eyebrow raised. "That was a nice clean shirt," she said. "Before you used it as a dust rag, that is."

Jen looked down. Sure enough, she looked as if she had been swept out from under the cabinet along with her yo-yo.

As Zeke pushed the hairy pile into a dustpan and headed for the kitchen, Jen raced through the dining room and into the lighthouse tower. Aunt Bee and Uncle Cliff had renovated the circular building so that she and Zeke could each have a bedroom in the tower. Jen's room was on the second floor; Zeke's was on the third. Both of their rooms were curved on one side with awesome views of the Atlantic Ocean and the bay just to the south.

Jen dashed through the Lighthouse Museum of Memorabilia that she and Zeke had set up on the first floor of the tower, then ran up one flight of circular stairs to her room. She flung open her door. The twins had helped Aunt Bee decorate all the guest rooms with flower themes, but Jen had decorated her own room, so instead of flowery wallpaper, posters of every possible sport covered her walls. Her favorite was a shot of two huge men who looked like sumo wrestlers playing tiddledywinks. Zeke's room, on the other hand, always made her laugh because it looked like a set from *Star Wars*.

Catching her breath, Jen put on a clean T-shirt. She threw her dusty shirt onto the pile of dirty clothes on the floor of her closet. She'd take them to the basement laundry room later, she decided as she shoved the closet doors shut and charged back downstairs.

Zeke was helping Aunt Bee refold one of the homemade quilts they kept draped over the backs of chairs and couches around the B&B. Suddenly he stopped folding and cocked his head. "Someone's coming."

Jen didn't hear anything, but she ran to the front door and threw it wide open. The cool, salty air blew in along with the sound of the Atlantic Ocean crashing against the rocky beach just below the bluff. It was rather warm for Maine at this time of year, but she wasn't complaining.

Sure enough, a small green car pulled up the circular driveway. A very tall woman with frizzy orange hair unfolded herself from the car. Her wide, freckled face looked upset.

Zeke hurried down the stairs to help her with her luggage, but the woman had already grabbed her suitcase from the trunk of the car and slammed it shut before Zeke reached her.

"I'll carry that for you," he offered.

"Oh, thank you," the woman said, handing over her suitcase with a shaking hand. "I'm Mrs. Adams." She reached into her car and snatched up her purse, along with a new toothbrush and box of toothpaste.

Aunt Bee stepped forward. "I'm Beatrice Dale, but please call me Bee. Come in and relax. Did you have a long trip?"

Jen moved out of the way as everyone walked into the foyer. She looked at Zeke struggling with the suitcase. Jen smiled because she knew exactly what Zeke was thinking. *Next time you get to carry the suitcase!* It wasn't uncommon for their thoughts to mix together. They often found themselves thinking the same thing. It was almost like *hearing* each other's thoughts.

Zeke and Jen caught up with their aunt and Mrs. Adams at the check-in desk.

They got there just in time to hear Mrs. Adams say, "And then it happened."

"What happened?" Aunt Bee asked as she wrote Mrs. Adams's name in the registry.

"Someone tried to kill me!"

Dead
Serious

"Wow!" Jen exclaimed just as Zeke asked, "How?"

"Look at my hands. They're still trembling."

The three of them looked. Sure enough, her hands were shaking.

"I'll get you some tea," Aunt Bee offered as she led Mrs. Adams to a chair. She went into the kitchen to heat some water.

"How did it happen?" Zeke asked.

"There's a terrible turn in the road along the coast, just before you get here—"

"That's called Dead Man's Curve," Jen interrupted.

The woman shuddered, and Zeke glared at his sister. Mrs. Adams was obviously upset enough without Jen adding to it. Sometimes Jen opened her mouth without thinking.

"And so, what happened?" he prodded gently.

Mrs. Adams took a deep, steadying breath. "Well, right before that curve is a little market called Quick Stop or something. I needed to stop there to get a couple of items I forgot." She motioned to the toothpaste and toothbrush still sitting on the check-in counter where she'd left them. "I was very careful pulling out of the parking lot. But as soon as I got to the first part of that dangerous curve, another car—a bright red car—hit me from behind. I skidded off the road and onto the tiny shoulder. I could have smashed through the guardrail, sailed over the cliff, and crashed down on the jagged rocks below."

"How awful!" Aunt Bee exclaimed, returning with a mug of cinnamon tea for the guest. "Were you hurt?"

"No, thank goodness," Mrs. Adams said as she gratefully clasped the steaming mug. "But my taillight was broken."

"I'm sure it was just an accident," Aunt Bee said.

"Then why didn't the other driver stop?" Mrs. Adams demanded. She shook her head, sending her orange hair bouncing back and forth. "No, that driver meant to hit me and leave me for dead. I'm sure of it."

Mrs. Adams sipped her tea. "Luckily, I was able to get back on the road and drive here. And to top everything off, I cut my finger. It probably happened when I got out to check my taillight." She held up the index finger of her right hand, which she'd wrapped in tissue.

At a nod from her aunt, Jen hurried to the powder room by the parlor to get Mrs. Adams a bandage.

"You should fill out a police report," Aunt Bee suggested, reaching for the phone that sat on one side of the front desk.

"Oh, no," Mrs. Adams protested. "I don't want to do that."

"But if you do," Zeke said, "the police might be able to find out who hit you."

"You could have been killed," Jen added, handing the bandage to Mrs. Adams. She shrugged when her brother and aunt glared at her.

"No, no," Mrs. Adams said. "I don't want to start off in this town with a complaint to the police, especially if I'm worthy enough to get the job." She sat up straighter. "We'll just try to forget this little incident ever happened. Everything will be fine." She smiled, but Zeke noticed her lips trembled. Mrs. Adams was obviously still upset, but he had to give her credit for being so brave.

"If you're sure," Aunt Bee said doubtfully. "Just let me know if you change your mind."

With that, Zeke carried her suitcase down the hall to her first-floor room while Mrs. Adams followed.

"You're in the Daffodil Den," he told her.

"What on earth does that mean?" she asked. But as soon as Zeke opened the door to her room, she breathed a sigh of appreciation.

Zeke grinned. Guests were always impressed by the rooms. Each one was decorated in a different flower theme. He thought the decorations were a bit overwhelming, but Aunt Bee loved her flowers and wanted everyone else to enjoy them, too.

"I just adore daffodils," Mrs. Adams gushed, surveying the room. "And look at that wonderful mobile."

Zeke glanced at the mobile of hanging ceramic daffodils. "One of the shops in town sells mobiles with everything from flowers to whales," he explained. "You'll have to check it out."

Mrs. Adams smiled and reached into her purse. "I certainly will. Thank you so much for your help."

Zeke returned to the foyer to tell Aunt Bee and Jen that Mrs. Adams was going to lie down and relax a bit before dinner. Then he flashed a dollar bill at Jen as Aunt Bee took the empty mug back to the kitchen.

She narrowed her eyes at him. It was always a contest to see who could get more tips.

Zeke tucked the bill into his pocket. "Do you think Mrs. Adams's car was hit by accident?"

"Why would someone purposely run her off the road?" Jen asked.

Instead of answering, Zeke pointed. "Look, Mrs. Adams forgot her toothbrush and toothpaste. I'd better bring them to her."

"I'll do it," Jen offered, but Zeke had already picked up the items.

"Forget it," Zeke said with a grin. "She's not going to tip you just for bringing these to her."

As Zeke walked down the hall he said over his shoulder, "The least they could have done was given her a bag for this stuff."

"It's better for the environment not to get a bag," she called after him, but he was too far away to hear her.

As Jen turned around, the front door banged open and a large bearded man stomped in. Jen hurried forward to take his suitcase, but he wouldn't let go of it.

"Hello," he announced in a hearty voice. "I'm Dr. Bowles."

Jen tried to take his suitcase a second time, but he pulled it out of her reach.

"I'll take care of this," he said. Although Dr. Bowles smiled when he talked, Jen could see he was dead serious. A shiver of unease tickled her spine.

"Now, that's strange," Dr. Bowles said as he walked over to the check-in desk and Aunt Bee hurried to stand behind it. "I know I had my wallet when I left." He patted his pockets several times and finally found it in the inside pocket of his jacket. He shook his head. "Ever since my wife died five years ago, I keep losing everything. She used to say if she wasn't around, I'd forget to screw my head on straight in the morning." He burst out laughing. "At least I didn't forget my head today!"

Jen glanced at Zeke, who had just come back from his delivery. *Okayyyy*, they both thought as they started to laugh. It was hard not to when Dr. Bowles was chuckling louder than a department store Santa Claus. He looked a little bit like one, too, with a big belly and a full salt-and-pepper beard. But even as she laughed, Jen couldn't forget the look he had given her when she had tried to carry his bag. *There's something weird about this guy*, she thought.

Just then, two more people entered the B&B. One was a thin man with slightly hunched shoulders and thinning brown hair who introduced himself as Mr. Crane. He clutched a well-worn briefcase with one clawlike hand. The other guest, a woman who introduced herself as Ms. Hartlet, wore a navy blue suit and a shy smile. She'd pulled her dark brown hair into a tight bun at the back of her head.

"I've heard of you," Dr. Bowles said to Mr. Crane.

"You're the principal at Kennedy Middle School in Lake Cove, Michigan. I've read all about your award-winning programs. You're doing a great job."

Zeke couldn't believe it when the thin man didn't even say thank you. He simply scowled at them all and shook his head as though he didn't like compliments. Zeke saw his sister was about to say something, but he jumped in before she could put her foot in her mouth.

"Would you like me to show you to your room, Mr. Crane?" Zeke asked. "You're on the second floor in the Hibiscus Hideaway."

The man rubbed his long pointed nose and said, "Fine."

They left, and a few minutes later, Jen led Ms. Hartlet upstairs to the Rose Room, and Aunt Bee pointed Dr. Bowles to the Violet Valley, right off the foyer.

"Oh, this is lovely," Ms. Hartlet said when Jen opened her door. "How pretty and cozy. I'm sure I'll be very comfortable." She handed Jen a crisp dollar bill.

Jen nodded her thanks. When she got downstairs, she nearly ran into her brother. She waved her tip in front of his nose.

"Boy, Mr. Crane never smiles," Zeke grumbled. "I don't think he's too happy about being here." He held up a quarter. "And he's not a big tipper."

"Jen? Zeke?" Aunt Bee called from the front desk.

The twins hurried over. In the foyer they saw a young man wearing a jogging suit and running shoes, surrounded by piles of luggage. Jen groaned inwardly and felt the same vibes from her brother. So much to carry. Ugh. No tip was worth it.

"Mr. Mitchell will be staying in the Orchid Oasis," Aunt Bee said, much to Jen's and Zeke's relief.

As the twins lugged his bags into the room closest to the entry foyer, Mr. Mitchell directed them. "Careful with that one," he ordered as Jen nearly broke her back trying to pick up one of the suitcases. "It's very important."

Zeke picked up a large bag that turned out to be rather light. He couldn't imagine what was in it, but he didn't think it would be polite to ask.

When they finally dragged the last bag into his room, Mr. Mitchell shut his door without even saying thank you. The twins flopped onto a pair of chairs.

"I'm glad the B&B isn't booked up this week; it looks like we'll have our hands full. I wonder what was in Mr. Mitchell's bags," Zeke said.

"I don't know," Jen said. "But it's pretty strange to have so much luggage for only five days."

"Hey, we've had weirder people than that stay here."

Jen laughed. "That's for sure! Remember the lady who brought all her pictures of her cats and insisted on showing them to everyone?"

"Over and over again," Zeke finished for her.

They both chuckled at the memory, then Zeke headed for his room. "I'm going to try out my new video game, the one with the snowboarders. Want to try it?"

Jen scrunched up her nose. "No, thanks. That game makes me dizzy. It's way too realistic. Anyway, I told Stacey I'd call her. We're going to kick around a soccer ball."

"Don't get beaned in the face," Zeke called over his shoulder as he took off.

"Don't fall off a mountain," Jen shouted back.

Jen and Zeke didn't see any of the candidates again until dinner. Aunt Bee served the evening meal family style, with everyone sitting on either side of the long dining room table. She served breakfast every day, but on special occasions she also served dinner. Tonight she'd made her famous spaghetti with meat sauce and a Caesar salad. The twins had been in charge of making a large basket of garlic bread.

As Dr. Bowles handed Mrs. Adams the bread, she

shuddered. "That's quite a ring you're wearing!"

Zeke looked at the large gold ring wrapped around Dr. Bowles's plump pinky. It was a serpent with two red eyes. Zeke thought it was pretty cool looking.

Dr. Bowles laughed. "You don't like snakes?"

"I hate them," she answered.

"I don't like them, either," Ms. Hartlet said from across the table. "They give me the creeps."

Jen noticed Mr. Crane shudder.

"They're so slimy," Mrs. Adams said.

"Actually," Zeke said, "they're not slimy at all. They're quite dry to the touch."

Mrs. Adams shivered. "Well, I don't intend to touch one, so I'll just have to take your word for it."

As they were finishing dinner, Aunt Bee announced that she locked the doors at eleven each night. "If any of you are out after that, simply come to my private entrance, the blue door with the wreath on it, and knock. I'll let you in."

"I think I'll go for a stroll along the bluff," Dr. Bowles said, rubbing his large stomach as he popped a last bite of buttery bread into his mouth. "I want to work off some of this delicious dinner."

"Strolling isn't going to do you much good," Mr. Mitchell said. "Running is much better exercise. That's what I'm going to do. Anyone want to come?"

"Strolling sounds better to me," Mrs. Adams said.

"Me, too," said Ms. Hartlet. She turned to Mr. Crane. "Would you like to join us?"

Mr. Crane scowled. "I should think not. I'm going to prepare for my interviews. After all, only *one* of us can get this job."

3

The Dragon Box

Jen squinted at the red digital clock radio next to her bed. She groaned. It wasn't even midnight, but something had woken her up. Slinky lay curled up next to her, purring softly, so it couldn't have been the cat. Was Woofer barking? She listened intently, but all she could hear was the crash of waves outside her window.

A tingle of unease ran across her shoulders. Zeke and Aunt Bee made fun of how deeply she slept. She could usually sleep through thunderstorms or Slinky walking on top of her.

She silently slipped out of bed and tiptoed to the window. Outside, the bright moon illuminated the ocean, making it glow with a silvery light. The yard looked deserted. From the other side of the room, she could look back toward the bay, but if she opened her window and leaned out, she could also see the far side of the parking lot over the roof of the B&B.

She stuck her head out the bay-side window and was breathing in the cool misty air when she saw something move out of the corner of her eye. Was that a person moving around the parking lot, or was it just a midnight shadow? It seemed that the harder she stared, the less she could see.

Her breath caught in her throat. Yes! There was someone snooping at the far end of the lot. Well, maybe not snooping, she decided. It was hard to tell what the person was doing from so far away. But why would anyone be in the parking lot at this time of night? Aunt Bee had already locked the doors, so whoever it was either didn't belong anywhere near here, or was a guest who was locked out of the B&B.

The shadowy figure disappeared again. Just when Jen was deciding she must have dreamed the whole thing, the person stepped back into sight, right in the bright moonlight. This time she recognized the bulky figure. Dr. Bowles!

When he disappeared from sight again a few seconds later, he didn't reappear. Jen pondered this as she snuggled back into bed. Before she came to any conclusions, she fell fast asleep. And this time, nothing woke her until Zeke banged on her door at six the next morning.

Before Jen had a chance to tell Zeke about the midnight prowler, Mr. Crane stormed into the dining room where everyone was already eating the steaming-hot blueberry muffins that Aunt Bee had just set out in a basket on the dining table.

"Who stole my briefcase?" Mr. Crane demanded. His pinched face and the scalp showing through his hair were red with anger. "I had it last night, and this morning it's gone!"

"Could you have left it somewhere?" Aunt Bee asked, concern in her voice.

Mr. Crane's lips thinned. "Absolutely not! All my important notes were in my briefcase. I didn't let it out of my sight for one second! Someone stole it right out of my room, and I demand to know who it was."

Everyone looked at one another.

Jen stared at Dr. Bowles. Did he look guilty, or was it her imagination?

"How on earth could someone steal it out of your room?" Mr. Mitchell asked, taking a large bite of muffin. "We all have locks on our doors."

Mr. Crane's eyes shifted for a second. Jen glanced at Zeke. She knew what he was thinking: Mr. Crane had forgotten to lock his door.

Ms. Hartlet quietly asked, "Surely you locked your door last night?"

Mr. Crane didn't answer right away. Then he said, "Of course I did. I'm not a fool."

Zeke and Jen looked at each other again, positive he was lying. Even so, if someone had stolen his briefcase, something very suspicious was going on.

"I'm sure we'll find it," Aunt Bee said, passing him the butter. "Why don't you have a muffin to start your day?"

"How can I possibly eat with such a catastrophe at hand?" With that he made an about-face and stalked out of the dining room.

"The poor man," Ms. Hartlet said softly. "He seems so upset. But I'm sure he's overprepared for these interviews. I see it in my top students all the time. Even the littlest quiz puts them in a tizzy."

Zeke knew exactly what she meant. Tests and quizzes were very important if he wanted to keep his grades up. He knew Jen didn't worry about them half as much as he did, yet she seemed to get exactly the same marks. That didn't seem fair to him at all.

Jen nudged him on the shoulder. It was time to walk to the bus stop at the bottom of the hill.

When they got outside, Jen grinned at her brother. "Can you imagine getting bent out of shape over a quiz?"

"Very funny," he said, laughing. Jen loved to tease him about how much he studied.

"Just kidding," Jen said. "But Mr. Crane sure was upset about his briefcase. You'd think he had gold hidden in there instead of some dumb old notes."

Zeke shook his head. "I can't believe someone actually sneaked into his room and stole it."

That reminded Jen about seeing Dr. Bowles last night, and by the time the bus picked them up, she had told her brother the whole story.

"Maybe you dreamed the whole thing. Dr. Bowles doesn't seem like a thief to me," Zeke said, sitting across the aisle from Jen, who sat down next to her best friend.

Stacey leaned over, her bright blond hair curling around her face. "Who's a thief?"

Jen and Zeke looked at each other, silently deciding it wasn't such a good idea to tell Stacey that a possible future principal might be a thief. The whole school would know by lunch.

"Oh, nobody," Zeke said nonchalantly. "Just something we saw on television last night."

Stacey made a face at him. "Yeah, right. Like you two ever watch TV."

The three of them laughed, knowing she was right, but at least it changed the subject for the rest of the ride.

As Jen and Zeke walked through the front doors of Mystic Middle School with their friends, a loud voice boomed, "There they are! The bed-and-breakfast twins!"

Jen lowered her head, her cheeks flaming. "This is not happening. How did they get here before us, anyway?"

"They weren't in a slow yellow school bus," Zeke answered, trying not to move his lips. He knew how good teachers were at reading lips.

"Jen! Zeke! Over here."

They had no choice but to look up and wave to Dr. Bowles. Mrs. Adams and Ms. Hartlet waved, too. Mr. Mitchell was too busy straightening his tie. Zeke couldn't believe he was wearing a pair of blue-and-white running shoes with his gray suit. Scowling as usual, Mr. Crane looked severe in his black suit, white shirt, and dark blue tie. He stuffed his hands into his pockets as though he didn't know what to do with them without a briefcase to hang on to.

Someone dug Zeke in the ribs and said, "Principal's pet!"

Zeke grinned at his friend Tommy. "I can't help it if they're staying at our B&B and they happen to think Jen and I are adorable." Laughing, he and Tommy headed for their homeroom.

Jen tried to slip by the B&B guests, but Mrs.

Adams stopped her with a cheery smile. "How are you this morning, my dear?" Mrs. Adams trilled as she fluffed her brightly colored hair.

"Fine," Jen mumbled. She could feel the other kids staring at her. "And you?" This was one of those times when she wished Aunt Bee hadn't taught them to be so polite.

"Wonderful, thank you." She took a deep breath through her nose. "Something about this Maine air. It's so fresh and invigorating."

Jen smiled and nodded, though all she could smell was chalk dust. She said good-bye and hurried away. Stacey caught up with her.

"Who are they?" Stacey asked.

"They're all interviewing to be the next principal, and they're staying at the B&B."

Stacey giggled. "Lucky you."

"Yeah, right!"

After school, Aunt Bee greeted the twins with freshly baked chocolate chip cookies. They both had homework to do, but first they needed to tidy the guests' rooms. That was their main job at the B&B and neither of the twins minded doing it. It was fun to see how the way the guests kept their rooms reflected their personalities.

They always cleaned the rooms in the same order, starting downstairs with the Daffodil Den, going up the back stairs to clean the upstairs rooms, then coming down the front stairs to clean the remaining two guest rooms. This week that meant starting in Mrs. Adams's room and ending with Dr. Bowles's room.

Slinky slunk into the Daffodil Den with them. While the twins dusted, swept, and put out clean towels, the cat pounced, pranced, and pawed at all the loose, dangling items.

Mrs. Adams's clothes were hung neatly, Jen noticed as she shut the closet door. Her clothes were all bright shades of red, orange, and yellow—just as colorful as her hair. She and her belongings went well with the room's yellow trimmings.

Zeke read the title of the novel on her bedside table. It was called *Murder at the Library* by Esther Barrimore, and it looked as if it had never even been opened.

Mrs. Adams had obviously picked some wild-flowers last night and put them in her drinking glass on the dresser. They looked very cheerful.

Jen chased Slinky out from under the bed, so they could move upstairs to Ms. Hartlet's room.

"Look," Zeke said. "She hardly unpacked." Two

almost identical-looking dark tailored suits hung in the closet. And one pair of dark low-heeled pumps stood primly on the closet floor.

"At least that keeps the room neat," Jen said, dusting the rosy pink windowsill. "Maybe she doesn't think she'll make it through all the interviews, so she doesn't want to get too comfortable."

"If that's the reason, she sure doesn't have much confidence in herself."

Jen moved on to dust the night table, where she noticed something was preventing the drawer from closing all the way. She opened the drawer an inch and discovered a pair of dark brown leather gloves. "How weird," she said, pointing. "Who wears gloves at this time of year?"

Zeke turned to her. "Hey, stop being so nosy. We'll never get finished at this rate."

With one last look at the gloves, Jen tucked them into the drawer and shut it all the way. Then she followed her brother out of the room.

Mr. Crane's room was also neat as a pin. Not a single thing was out of place. There were no shoes lying around, no loose ties, no books on the bedside table. Slinky jumped onto the dresser and knocked over the only personal possession Jen could see in the entire room.

Jen picked up the framed photo of a plump

woman with curly hair and a wide smile and set it gently back on the dresser.

"I like rooms like this," Zeke said as he shut the door and locked it behind them.

"That's just because you're a neat freak," Jen teased.

They went down the front stairs and opened the door to Mr. Mitchell's room. They were shocked at the sight of it.

"You should feel right at home in this mess," Zeke jeered, staring around with a mixture of disgust and amazement.

"Hey, even I'm not *this* bad," Jen retorted.

The floor was littered with jogging suits, sneakers, dumbbells, and an exercise mat. Magazines covered his unmade bed: *Sports Illustrated*, *Men's Health*, *Karate Magazine*, and many others. With a groan, they started stacking the magazines on the table by the window. After they had made the bed, they placed the dumbbells in a neat row against one wall and the shoes against another.

"He has *five* pairs of running shoes," Jen said, amazed.

When they finally finished, they heaved a sigh of relief and headed for the Violet Valley. As they walked down the hall, lugging their cleaning supplies, Mrs. Adams slipped out of Dr. Bowles's room, closing the door quietly behind her.

"Hi," Zeke said.

Mrs. Adams whirled around. "Oh, I didn't hear you coming."

"Did you need something?" Jen asked, trying not to sound suspicious.

"I just got back and thought I'd look around this lovely old house." She shrugged slightly. "Of course, as soon as I realized this was a guest room, I came out. I adore the way you've decorated each room in a different flower theme."

"Aunt Bee is in charge of the decorating," Jen said. She held up a bucket of cleaning supplies. "We're in charge of the cleaning."

Mrs. Adams laughed as she walked away. The twins let themselves into Dr. Bowles's room, relieved that he kept his room rather neat.

"Wow, look at this cool box," Jen exclaimed.

Zeke came closer to the dresser and stared at the wooden box, which had an intricately carved dragon on it. "This is strange," he said, pointing to the initials above the lock.

"M. C. R.," Jen read out loud. "Those aren't his initials—his last name is Bowles."

Suddenly, the twins heard a noise behind them. Dr. Bowles had stepped into the room and was staring openmouthed at the twins. He immediately snatched the box off the dresser. Zeke heard something inside it rattle.

Dr. Bowles glared at the twins. "Don't ever, ever touch that box again."

"We didn't touch it," Jen protested. "We only—"

But Dr. Bowles cut her short. "Just get out of here. If I ever catch you snooping around in here again, I'll tell your aunt!"

4
Whatever
It Takes

"Dr. Bowles is like Dr. Jekyll and Mr. Hyde," Jen said under her breath as they carried the cleaning supplies back to the kitchen pantry. "One minute he's Mister Jolly, and the next he's about to rip off our heads."

Zeke nodded. "There must be something important about that box. I heard rattling when he grabbed it."

"Maybe it's diamonds or something."

"Sure," Zeke said with a sarcastic edge to his voice. "Mr. Crane has gold in his briefcase and Dr. Bowles has diamonds in his box." He shook his head. "Where do you come up with these ideas anyway?"

Jen grinned. "Wait till you hear what I think about the others."

Zeke groaned. "I'm not sure I want to hear this." But when Jen didn't say anything, he added, "Okay, tell me."

Jen dropped the bucket in the corner of the pantry and leaned the broom against the wall. She turned to her twin and ticked off the guests on her fingers. "We've done Bowles and Crane. Then there's Adams and her frizzy orange hair that is too wild to be believed. I think it's really a wig and she's an undercover spy on a mission to catch Mr. Crane and Dr. Bowles."

Zeke rolled his eyes. "She's not exactly my idea of a secret agent."

"That's why she would be so perfect for the job. No one would suspect her. Mr. Mitchell is on the run from the police, which is why he wears running shoes all the time. He can make a quick getaway. And Ms. Hartlet is . . ." Her voice trailed off as she stared at the ceiling, thinking.

"Don't tell me you haven't figured her out yet," Zeke said as they settled at the kitchen table with some drinks.

Jen sipped on her tall glass of lemonade, then leaned forward and lowered her voice. "Ms. Hartlet is probably the most dangerous of them all because she seems so innocent."

"You're nuts," Zeke said, waving his glass of milk and nearly sloshing half of it on the table.

Jen shrugged and sat back casually. "Maybe, maybe not."

Once the guests had left for their dinner with the superintendent of schools, Jen and Zeke sat down with Aunt Bee in the kitchen. When it was just the three of them, they ate at the small round table in the cozy kitchen.

The kitchen was one of Jen's favorite rooms. Aunt Bee collected all sorts of bee knickknacks. She had covered the fridge with bee magnets and hung bee-patterned curtains at the kitchen window. There were also bee-shaped pot holders and cushions, bee figurines, and bee note cards. Postcards featuring bees that her friends had sent her were taped to the cabinets. Aunt Bee even had a hive-shaped telephone with a large bee for the hand piece.

Jen liked to tease her aunt by saying the kitchen was *bee-eautiful.*

"Why are you so tired tonight?" Zeke asked his aunt as he scraped the last bit of chocolate cream pie off his plate. "You've been yawning all through dinner."

"I didn't get much sleep last night," Aunt Bee admitted, getting up to do the dishes. "Dr. Bowles knocked on my door at eleven-forty-five. I can't imagine what he was doing out so late, but he said he simply lost track of the time out on the bluff."

Jen looked at her brother and lifted her eyebrows. So she hadn't been dreaming after all.

"That's weird," Zeke said.

Aunt Bee shrugged. "I did stay up awhile wondering about it, which is why I'm so tired today."

"We'll take the garbage out for you," Zeke said.

"We will?" Jen countered.

Zeke gave her a "just do it" stare.

The twins each picked up a large black bag stuffed with garbage and headed outside to the bins they kept on the parking lot side of the B&B.

Slinky wound between Zeke's feet as he walked, almost tripping him. "Scoot!" he said, but the cat ignored him and gave his ankles one last rub before prancing ahead of them. She made it to the garbage bins before them, and by the time they'd caught up, she'd found something to play with.

Zeke hefted his bag over the top of a bin and Jen did the same.

They stood for a moment laughing at Slinky, who tumbled and pounced at a scrap of red plastic.

"You'd think it was a mouse, the way she's enjoying herself," Zeke commented. "Where did she get that piece of broken plastic anyway?"

"Beats me." Jen lunged for the cat, but Slinky

playfully darted away, the plastic piece clamped between her sharp little teeth.

As they were returning to the back entrance of the B&B, Zeke said, "I wonder what Dr. Bowles was doing last night—"

Jen grabbed his arm, her mind no longer on Dr. Bowles. "Look!" She pointed to one of the parked cars. The guests had gone to dinner in two cars, leaving three behind. "That red car. It has a bashed-in front fender!"

In the fading daylight, they hurried over to the car and crouched in front of it, examining the damage. The fender was crumpled and red paint had chipped off in places, leaving rusty brown marks.

"I'll bet it was this car that almost ran Mrs. Adams over the cliff!"

Zeke agreed. "But whose is it?"

The twins raced inside to check the registration cards Aunt Bee kept behind the check-in desk.

"Here it is," Zeke said.

Jen read over his shoulder. "Mr. Mitchell!"

They heard footsteps and voices on the front porch and quickly put away the metal file box.

The twins watched Mr. Mitchell enter the B&B, tugging on his tie to loosen it. Jen nudged her brother in the ribs and whispered, "Do you think he tried to run Mrs. Adams off the road?"

As though Mr. Mitchell had heard her, he stared back at the twins with narrowed eyes. Jen gave him a small smile and waved. Mr. Mitchell didn't wave or smile back.

When he turned away from them, Zeke said softly, "He sure looks guilty."

Just then, Dr. Bowles burst through the front door holding a briefcase over his head. "I've found it!" he shouted.

Mr. Crane whirled around. "That's my briefcase!" He lunged forward. "Where was it?" he demanded as Dr. Bowles handed it over.

"Just next to the porch in those bushes. I saw the cat duck in there, and when I looked closer, there it was. The cat was sitting on it."

"Slinky found the briefcase?" Jen asked.

Dr. Bowles nodded. "Looked that way to me."

"That's ridiculous," Mr. Crane nearly spat out. "And I suppose you're going to tell me that the cat put it there, too." With one hand he held up the case, and with the other he twirled the numbered lock and opened it. He quickly rifled through the papers, looked satisfied, and closed the briefcase with a sharp click.

"It's a relief that you have it back," Aunt Bee said.

Mr. Crane opened his mouth as though he was

going to say something, but the tinkle of piano keys coming from the parlor cut him off. The twins followed the sound with the other guests.

Mrs. Adams sat on the piano bench, humming as she played. Aunt Bee kept the old upright piano tuned, even though Jen and Zeke had stopped taking lessons last year.

"Let's sing some songs," Mrs. Adams suggested, her fingers running gracefully across the keys despite the bandage on her right forefinger.

The twins looked at each other. *Songs? Did Mrs. Adams think this was camp?*

"Not for me," Mr. Crane said stiffly. "I have work to do." He shook his briefcase for emphasis.

Dr. Bowles laughed. "Oh, stay, it'll do you good to relax. Don't be a hermit."

Mr. Crane frowned, but he stayed, sitting stiffly on a side chair.

Jen and Zeke shared a seat in the corner where they had a good view of the room—especially of Mr. Mitchell.

Aunt Bee entered the parlor and walked over to Ms. Hartlet. "This came in the mail for you today."

Ms. Hartlet took the letter with a surprised "Thank you."

As Mrs. Adams began to play "Michael, Row Your Boat Ashore," Jen watched Ms. Hartlet. She looked worried as she opened the envelope and unfolded a letter.

Even from across the room, Jen could see Ms. Hartlet heave a heavy sigh as she read it. Then she started to sing halfheartedly as she absently shredded the letter.

After three songs, Mr. Crane stood up abruptly and stomped out of the room, hugging his briefcase to his chest as though he was afraid someone would snatch it from him.

Soon the other guests trickled out of the room as well. Before she left, Ms. Hartlet gathered up the slips of paper that she had torn.

Only Jen, Zeke, and Aunt Bee remained.

Aunt Bee yawned. "I'm going to lock up early tonight since everyone is already in. And then I'm going to bed!" She looked at her watch. "It's time for you two to hit the sack, too."

"We will," Zeke said as their aunt left the room. Then he turned to Jen. "Did you see him do anything suspicious?"

"Who?"

Zeke groaned. "Mr. Mitchell. Remember?"

"I remember," Jen said defensively. "I just forgot

for a second. Anyway, I didn't see him do or say anything suspicious. Did you?"

Zeke shook his head and stood up to leave.

"I'm just going to look for Slinky," Jen said. She liked to take Slinky to her room at night. The affectionate cat slept at the foot of her bed and woke her up at the same time every morning by gently purring in her ear.

Jen poked around the room, looking in all of Slinky's usual hiding spots.

She was about to give up when she saw a scrap of paper under a chair. Realizing it was a piece of the letter Ms. Hartlet had torn to pieces, she picked it up. Only a few scrawled words were visible.

Forgetting about Slinky, Jen charged out of the room and raced after Zeke. He was in the dining room, straightening the chairs for tomorrow's breakfast.

"Look!" She held the paper out to him.

Zeke read out loud: "'And do whatever it takes to get the job, because . . .'" He turned the paper over. "That's it? What is this? What does it mean?"

Jen explained about Ms. Hartlet's letter and how she had torn it up as though she didn't want anyone to read it.

"Seems really suspicious," Zeke agreed, shaking his head.

"Suspicious how?" Jen asked. She had been think-ing the same thing, but it didn't make sense.

A sudden shout startled the twins. It was followed by three loud thumps as though someone was falling down the stairs!

5
Mighty Suspicious

Jen and Zeke tore into the foyer and looked up the wide front stairs. About halfway down, Mr. Mitchell was slowly easing himself onto his feet.

Aunt Bee appeared in her fluffy green bathrobe, her long hair loose down her back. "What happened?"

Mr. Mitchell stretched his arms as if he was checking for broken bones. "Someone pushed me down the stairs!"

"Surely not," Dr. Bowles said. He and the other guests had rushed out of their rooms and now crowded at both ends of the stairs.

"Then how did I fall?" Mr. Mitchell demanded.

"Perhaps you tripped," Ms. Hartlet suggested.

"Perhaps you pushed me," Mr. Mitchell shot back. "I am not out of shape and clumsy like some people here."

"What makes you think someone pushed you?"

Zeke asked before anyone could open their mouth to protest.

Mr. Mitchell stomped down the stairs. "I felt a hand shove me from behind. Luckily I'm in excellent physical condition and caught myself halfway down. I could have broken my neck!"

"What were you doing upstairs anyway?" Jen asked. She knew she sounded a little rude, but it was pretty strange for him to be on the second floor when his room was on the first.

"I was looking for my stopwatch. It's disappeared."

"And you thought it would be up here?" Mr. Crane asked from the top of the stairs. "Did you think one of us had stolen it?"

"*Somebody* took it," Mr. Mitchell snapped back.

"Now, now," Aunt Bee said soothingly. "I'm sure we'll find it. We do have a mischievous ghost who sometimes hides things. It'll turn up tomorrow. You'll see."

Zeke watched Ms. Hartlet at the top of the stairs, where she stood looking down. Her room was down the hall. Could she have pushed Mr. Mitchell and then ducked around the corner and into her room before anyone saw her?

When they were sure Mr. Mitchell wasn't injured, everyone said good night again. Jen and Zeke heard the locks click after each door shut.

The twins hugged their aunt and headed into the lighthouse tower to their rooms.

"Do you think it was an accident?" Jen asked Zeke.

"I don't know. He said he felt a hand on his back."

"What was he doing upstairs anyway? Did he really lose his stopwatch, or was that just an excuse to be up there?"

"If he did lose it," Zeke said, "why would it be on the second floor?"

The next day, during language arts, Jen ran an errand to the office for Mrs. Hay, her teacher. As she stood at the front desk, waiting for the secretary, she noticed that Mr. Crane was talking on the office phone. Jen edged toward him. *It's not that I'm nosy,* she told herself. *Just curious.*

Mr. Crane hunched over the phone. He obviously didn't want anyone to overhear him.

What could possibly be so important and private? Jen wondered.

"I just can't," Mr. Crane said hoarsely into the mouthpiece. He said something else, but it was too soft to hear.

Jen inched closer, her mouth going dry when she

heard Mr. Crane's next few words.

"I can't do it. These people are so . . . It's harder than I thought it would be . . . Didn't go as planned, and neither did the other . . ."

The school secretary startled Jen by asking her what she wanted. By the time she'd finished talking to the secretary, Mr. Crane had left the office.

Jen was dying to tell Zeke what she'd overheard, but it was an hour until lunch, so she went back to class. Finally, the hour passed and Jen found Zeke in the cafeteria, but it was hard to talk over all the noise.

"That sounds suspicious," Zeke said after they had found a quieter corner.

Jen nodded, taking a bite of her peanut butter and banana sandwich.

"Suspicious how?"

"Offf hutting fe offers," Jen said.

Zeke rolled his eyes. "Try swallowing first," he advised.

"Of hurting the others," Jen said again after she'd washed down her bite with some ice-cold milk. "If he can get rid of the other candidates, he'll get the job! Remember, he was the one who pointed out that only one of them could be the principal. He must want it so badly he's willing to do anything to get the others out of the way."

Zeke nodded thoughtfully, chewing a bite of his homemade granola bar.

Before either of them had a chance to say anything more, Stacey appeared with a tray balanced in one hand. She tugged on Jen's arm. "Come on, Jen, you said you'd sit near the windows with me. You won't believe what Josh just told me!"

With a shrug at her brother, Jen stood up and hurried after her friend. She silently sent a message to Zeke. *We'll talk after school.* He must have gotten the message, because when she turned around to look at him, he nodded.

After the school bus dropped them off at the bottom of the hill, the twins trudged up the road to the B&B. "Did you have any brilliant thoughts?" Jen asked.

"About what?"

"About what's going on. There's too much weird stuff happening for it to all be coincidental, don't you think?"

"Maybe."

"What do you mean, maybe?" Jen demanded.

"Maybe we're just overreacting."

"Mr. Mitchell was almost killed falling down the

stairs and Mrs. Adams was practically run over, and you think I'm overreacting?" Jen huffed. "Maybe you're just *under*reacting!"

"There's no such word as underreacting," Zeke said.

Jen glared at him. "Oh, forget it. I'll figure this out on my own."

Inside, they found Detective Wilson sitting at the kitchen table with Aunt Bee. They were laughing over something, and Detective Wilson was finishing off a slice of apple pie à la mode.

Though the detective was retired now, he'd worked on the Mystic police force for forty years, and everyone still called him Detective Wilson. Jen thought he had a crush on Aunt Bee, but Zeke said he just liked her cooking. Either way, they were always glad to see him. He often came for snacks or dinner, and he liked to help Bee with the heavier work around the B&B.

He greeted them now with a smile warm enough to melt any ice cream left on his plate. Of course, there wasn't any ice cream left, Jen noted. When Aunt Bee cooked or baked, there was never anything left on anyone's plate.

Jen plunked down in a chair next to Detective Wilson. "Did Aunt Bee tell you about the accidents?"

The detective raised his eyebrows. "Accidents?"

"It was nothing," Aunt Bee assured him. "That's all they were—*accidents*."

"Maybe," Jen said, "but maybe not." She proceeded to tell the detective about Mrs. Adams's car accident and about Mr. Mitchell claiming to be pushed down the stairs and nearly breaking his neck.

"And don't forget Mr. Crane's missing briefcase," Zeke added.

Detective Wilson listened thoughtfully, then said, "I'm afraid there's nothing the police can do about those incidents unless the victims want to report them. Besides, they do sound like accidents. Even if Mrs. Adams and Mr. Mitchell made reports, it's likely nothing would come of them. And since Mr. Crane found his briefcase . . ." His voice trailed off and he shrugged.

Jen scowled at Zeke, who was giving her a smug smile. Aunt Bee got up and served each of the twins a slice of pie and said, "You'll need to wait to clean the rooms this afternoon. The guests are all resting right now. They have a dinner tonight and a big day of interviews tomorrow. I think the stress is getting to them."

Aunt Bee scooped out a big spoonful of ice cream for Jen. Just as she dropped it onto Jen's piece of pie, a bloodcurdling scream echoed through the B&B.

6

Another Victim

A chilling shiver snaked up Jen's spine. "Who was that?" she whispered.

The scream came again.

Detective Wilson was already on his feet, racing toward the sound. Jen, Zeke, and Aunt Bee followed close behind. They heard a commotion on the second floor and ran up the front stairs. Some of the guests were crowded in the hall outside Ms. Hartlet's room. Ms. Hartlet stood in the middle of the group, her hands over her face as Mrs. Adams tried to comfort her.

"What happened?" Detective Wilson asked.

"A s-s-snake," Ms. Hartlet said through chattering teeth.

Jen and Zeke pushed through the group and

stopped in the doorway. Dr. Bowles was on his hands and knees, looking for the snake under the bed.

"Have you seen it?" Zeke asked.

"Yep," Dr. Bowles grunted. "But it slithered away. Now I can't find it."

"What kind is it?"

"Just the innocent garden variety. Nothing to worry about."

"I'm not worried," Zeke said. "I'll help you look for it."

Jen joined the search. She didn't love snakes, but at least she knew this one wasn't poisonous. As she crawled around on the floor she thought, *That snake didn't get in here on its own. Something is definitely going on.*

She found the snake curled around the base of the wastebasket, right near the heater. After swallowing .a little screech, she called to Zeke and Dr. Bowles. She tried to keep her voice steady. "I found it."

Dr. Bowles scooped up the snake with one hand. The other guests gave him a lot of space as he exited Ms. Hartlet's room.

"Just a cute little garter snake," Dr. Bowles said with a hearty chuckle as he made his way down the stairs to bring the snake outdoors. Halfway down, he passed Mr. Mitchell and thrust the snake toward him. "Would you like to take it outside?"

Mr. Mitchell lurched back so far that Jen was sure he was about to fall backward over the banister. When he righted himself, she had to bite her lip to keep from laughing out loud.

"No, thanks," Mr. Mitchell said, still leaning away from the snake. "Looks like you have everything under control."

Dr. Bowles grinned. "If you're sure." He proceeded down the rest of the stairs and out the front door, chuckling the whole way.

Mr. Mitchell stared after him with his eyes narrowed and his lips pulled into a slash of annoyance.

If looks could kill, Zeke couldn't help thinking.

Ms. Hartlet had to be reassured several times that there weren't any more snakes in her room before she would go back in. Mr. Crane, whose room was across the hall, looked a little pale—especially when Mrs. Adams said, "I certainly hope there aren't snakes in any other rooms!"

Aunt Bee cleared her throat. "I can't imagine how the snake got in here, but there must be a logical explanation. This has never happened before."

Jen pulled on Zeke's arm, leading him downstairs and into the parlor. "See?" she hissed. "Something strange *is* going on. Someone tried to run Mrs. Adams off the cliff at Dead Man's Curve, someone stole Mr.

Crane's briefcase with all his important papers inside, someone shoved Mr. Mitchell down the stairs so that he almost broke his neck, and Ms. Hartlet was scared stiff."

Zeke nodded. "Maybe it isn't all so coincidental after all."

"Not only that," Jen said, "but the person responsible has to be someone staying here."

"Why?"

"Aunt Bee would have noticed a stranger coming in to drop off the snake. And last night she had locked up before Mr. Mitchell was pushed down the stairs. Obviously, someone wants the job so bad they're trying to scare away the competition."

"You're right," Zeke agreed.

"So we have to figure out who's causing all these accidents before someone gets hurt."

"But I'm sure Detective Wilson is going to do that."

Jen flopped on the couch with a little groan. "Who knows more about the guests? Detective Wilson or us? We'll figure out who it is and then tell him."

"Just a little sleuthing, right?"

"Exactly," Jen agreed. "So where do we start?"

"We'll have to examine the scene of each accident. Let's start with the first one and go from there."

Jen cringed. "That means we have to go to Dead Man's Curve!"

7

Dead Man's Curve

"Right. Dead Man's Curve," Zeke repeated. That dangerous S-turn in the road always gave him the willies. Calling it Dead Man's Curve, as the locals did, didn't help any. There were tons of accidents there each year. The city had recently repaved the road and put up a new guardrail, hoping to avoid more accidents. Obviously it hadn't worked—Mrs. Adams had had the first accident since they had improved the road.

"We'll go tomorrow," Jen said. "The teachers are having that in-service conference all day, so we'll be free to investigate."

"Did I hear you say you'll be free tomorrow?" Aunt Bee asked, stepping into the parlor. "Have you forgotten about painting the molding around the windows in the dining room and parlor?"

"But that could take all day," Jen wailed.

Aunt Bee winked at her. "You can start now if you'd like." With a grin, she left.

Jen and Zeke looked at each other. They didn't relish the idea of starting now, but what about their trip to Dead Man's Curve?

"We have to go look for clues right now," Jen said, looking at her watch.

"But it'll be getting dark soon."

"Not for at least another hour. Come on." She stood up.

Aunt Bee stepped back into the parlor. "I need you to help me in the kitchen for a while, Jen. No offense, Zeke, but your sister is better at kneading dough. All those years of playing softball have given her the strong hands needed for dough. Get it? Kneaded? Needed?" She grinned so wide her silver fillings shone.

Still grinning, she left again and Jen looked at her twin. "You'll just have to go to Dead Man's Curve alone."

Zeke swallowed hard. "Alone?" he repeated.

Jen nodded. "Can you think of another idea? I have to stay here and help Aunt Bee now, and tomorrow we have tons of work. This will be our—I mean *your* only chance."

"I guess so," Zeke said reluctantly, trying to think of another plan.

"You do want to solve this mystery, don't you?" Jen asked.

"Of course, but—"

"Then get going. Ride your bike and just be careful when you get to Dead Man's Curve."

"Gee, thanks for the advice," Zeke said, rolling his eyes.

As they left the parlor, Zeke looked around. He could have sworn he'd heard the creak of a footstep out here a second ago, but no one was in sight. He shrugged it off, figuring it must have been Aunt Bee.

Jen walked with him back to where they kept their bikes. She watched as her twin covered his wavy brown hair with a bright red helmet.

"Good luck," she said.

"Thanks." With that, Zeke pedaled off down the hill. He rode on the right side of the road—"with traffic," although there were very few cars.

Going downhill was easy. Zeke let the bike coast along. He tried not to think about Dead Man's Curve. But the more he tried not to think about it, the more he *did* think about it. *Dead Man's Curve. Dead Man's Curve. Dead Man's Curve. Argh!*

When the sloping road from the lighthouse leveled out, Zeke had to start pedaling. The sun was low in the sky behind the pine trees to his right as he

headed south. At least the dreaded curve in the road wasn't too far away. He figured he should be able to get there and back to the B&B within thirty to forty-five minutes tops.

He pedaled faster. Not that he was eager to get there, he just wanted to get this over with. As he neared the curve, his fingers gripped the handlebars tighter and tighter.

The road eased around a gentle turn, and then it suddenly bent into Dead Man's Curve. On the other side of the road was some grass, then a railing, and then nothing. The cliff dropped off to the smashing waves and sharp rocks below. This side of the road was hilly and shadowed by pine trees. Zeke rode on the dirt shoulder, staying as far from the pavement as possible. A few cars passed him, but they all moved at a safe speed, wisely heeding the yellow arrows and the signs that read SLOW DOWN, DANGEROUS CURVE AHEAD.

At last he reached the spot where, from her description, Mrs. Adams had been run off the road. He got off his bike and then very carefully walked with it across both lanes. He parked it in a ditch, avoiding the sheer drop right beside him, on the other side of the guardrail. He tried not to look over the edge. *It's not that I'm afraid of heights*, he told himself, *it's just that*—his mind went blank. *Okay, so I don't like heights*, he thought. He hated to admit it, even to himself.

Trying to ignore the cliff and the crashing waves below, Zeke began to look around for clues. Strong gusts of wind battered him, rustling the trees and blowing loose soil into his eyes. Squinting, he examined the road from where he stood. He didn't see any skid marks, which was a little strange. Maybe Mrs. Adams had exaggerated about how bad her accident had been.

Next he looked for pieces of plastic from the broken taillight, but with the wind blowing every which way, he wasn't surprised not to see any on the road. He got down on his hands and knees and checked in the grass along the side of the road by the guardrail. All he found was a 1950 nickel, a soda can, two old shoes that didn't match, and a marble. No bits of broken taillight.

Finally Zeke gave up. Sitting back on his heels, he looked around, wondering if he'd missed a spot. The sun hadn't set yet, but it was hidden behind the pine trees on the other side of the road. Zeke shivered and zipped up his jacket. It was getting darker and windier by the second. He hated to leave without finding anything important, but Aunt Bee didn't like either of the twins to be out after dark on their bikes.

He walked back to his bike, kicking the grass along

the way. He hoped to see the glint of broken pieces of red or white plastic. Something caught his eye, but when he bent closer to look, it was only a rusty scrap of metal. The sun was setting behind the pine trees and it was getting hard to see much of anything.

Suddenly, the roar of a car engine thundered behind him. He felt as if he were caught in a slow-motion movie as he turned around. Two giant glowing headlights had crossed the center line and were headed right for him! Without thinking, he jumped out of the way. He landed in the grass, twisting his right ankle. Then he tumbled to the ground. A sharp pain jabbed up his leg.

At the last possible second, the car swerved away from him and whizzed around the curve on screeching tires. The next second it was out of sight.

Zeke clutched his sore ankle. *What am I going to do now?* he wondered. No way could he ride his bike home, but Aunt Bee would kill him if she knew what had happened. He had to get home, no matter how much his ankle hurt.

He tried to calm down, but his heart wouldn't stop hammering behind his ribs.

Only one thought kept racing through his mind. Someone had tried to kill him. What if that someone came back to finish the job?

8

No Clue

Jen looked at her watch again, then glanced out the large kitchen window. It was nearly dark and Zeke had been gone for over an hour. He should have been back by now.

"What on earth are you doing?" Aunt Bee asked, peering over her niece's shoulder.

Jen looked down at the dough she was supposed to be kneading. But instead of pushing it this way and that, punching it, and throwing it down on the table as she was supposed to do, she had torn off little pieces and rolled them into balls the size of marbles.

"Sorry," Jen said, quickly trying to mush the dough back together again. "I guess I was distracted."

"By what?"

"Zeke should have been back by now," Jen blurted out.

"Back from where?"

"He—he went to Dead Man's Curve."

"At this time of day?" Aunt Bee asked, starting to untie her bee-dotted apron. "It's nearly dark. That's a dangerous piece of road, especially at twilight."

"I know," Jen said, rubbing dough off her fingers. "I'm worried about him."

Aunt Bee grabbed a large set of keys that hung from a peg. "Come on. We'd better go find him."

Jen ran after her aunt, and they buckled up in Aunt Bee's station wagon. They zoomed down the hill and along the coast road to Dead Man's Curve.

Glancing to the side, Jen saw that her aunt's lips were pressed into a thin line.

"I'm sorry," she said, her voice barely loud enough to be heard over the sound of the engine.

"You two should know better than to go to such a dangerous piece of road at sunset. Dusk is the worst possible time for drivers. It's hard to see."

Jen gripped the edges of her seat. She tried to focus in on Zeke. But as hard as she concentrated, all she felt was a sudden jab of pain in her ankle, which couldn't possibly mean anything. Or could it?

"There he is!" Jen shouted as they neared Dead Man's Curve.

Aunt Bee put on the brakes and carefully pulled to the side of the road, leaving the car lights on to warn any other traffic. The headlights shone on Zeke. He was pushing his bike and limping along beside it.

Jen and Aunt Bee hurried to meet him.

"Zeke, what happened?" Aunt Bee asked.

"It's your ankle, isn't it?" Jen said, suddenly realizing why she'd gotten the pain in her ankle when she was trying to connect with her brother.

Zeke nodded. "I twisted my ankle. I don't think it's broken, though."

"Let's get you home," Aunt Bee said. She helped her nephew to the car, while Jen rolled his bike over to it. They put the bike in the back and Zeke sprawled across the rear seat.

"I thought you guys would never come," he said once they were back on the road.

"We came as soon as Jennifer told me where you were and that you were late," Aunt Bee said.

Jen looked over the back of the seat at Zeke. They knew Aunt Bee was upset whenever she used their full names.

Slowly and carefully, Aunt Bee eased the large car around the tricky corners of Dead Man's Curve.

Jen fidgeted in the front seat. She had a feeling something major had happened to Zeke. There were so many questions she wanted to ask her brother, but not in front of their aunt. Aunt Bee would only worry and tell them not to get involved.

When they reached Quick Stop Mart, Aunt Bee pulled into the parking lot and handed Jen some money. "We're low on ice cream."

Jen hopped out and dashed into the store. She grabbed a gallon of vanilla and took it to the checkout counter.

"Hey, Jen," the clerk said.

Jen smiled at her best friend's older brother. "Hi, Brian. Do you like your new job?"

"It's okay," he said, ringing up her purchase. "Sometimes it's hard to get here on time, but I like payday, that's for sure!"

Jen laughed and shook her head when he offered her a red-white-and-blue-striped plastic bag for the ice cream. "I'm trying to save the environment. See you later, Brian."

She hopped in the car and Aunt Bee pulled out, heading toward home.

Jen held her breath as they once again negotiated the hairpin turns. Only this time she could look down the cliff on her right to the inky blackness of the ocean roaring beneath them. It seemed like they all breathed easier once they were past Dead Man's Curve.

When they reached the B&B, Aunt Bee turned to them before getting out of the car. "I don't know what you two are getting into," she said sternly. "But I want you both to be more careful. Do you understand?"

Zeke and Jen nodded solemnly.

Aunt Bee helped Zeke into the parlor where he could put ice on his ankle and eat dinner.

It wasn't until after they'd eaten that Jen had a chance to talk to Zeke alone. "So what happened out there?" she asked.

"A car almost hit me. I hurt my ankle jumping out of the way."

"What?! Was it an accident, or did someone try to hit you?" she asked.

Zeke shook his head. "The car came pretty close. Too close. It either meant to hit me, or scare me over the edge of the cliff."

"You must have been scared stiff."

"Nah," Zeke said. "It was nothing."

Jen narrowed her eyes at her twin.

Zeke grinned. "Okay, maybe a little scared," he admitted with a laugh. "That's the one bad thing about being a twin," he added. "I can't get anything past you!"

Jen laughed, too, realizing how relieved she was that her brother was back at home, safe and sound. "So what does it mean? Why did someone try to ki— hurt you?" She just couldn't say *kill*.

"I have no idea," Zeke admitted. "Maybe we know

something we're not supposed to know and one of the guests is getting nervous."

They thought for a moment in silence. Then Jen said, "What did the car that tried to hit you look like?"

"I don't know," Zeke admitted. "It all happened so fast. At the last moment I saw the car speed off around the corner, but it was too fast and too dark to see it."

"That means it could have been anyone."

"Oh, great. Someone is trying to get rid of us because we know too much, and we don't have a clue!"

The next morning, Zeke's ankle was feeling better.

"Good," Jen said. "You can help paint the window trim."

"I don't know if it feels good enough for all that work."

Jen glared at her twin. "It's going to feel a lot worse if you *don't* help me," she threatened.

"Ooooh, my little sister is going to hurt me."

Jen took a swipe at him, but even with a slightly sprained ankle, he was too quick. He hopped away, laughing.

Aunt Bee set them up in the dining room, assigning Zeke work he could do mostly sitting down and giving Jen the upper areas.

They finally finished around noon.

"Can you put everything away?" Zeke asked. "My ankle is kind of throbbing again."

Jen eyed her brother, trying to figure out if he was just trying to get out of more work. He did look a little pale. "Don't worry. I'll do it."

She piled all the paint cans and brushes into a box and headed out the back door where she passed Mr. Mitchell coming in. He looked startled to see her.

Jen smiled. "Hi. Can I help you with something?" She hadn't meant to sound nosy, but the way Mr. Mitchell's face turned red, she got the feeling she had asked the wrong question.

"No, thanks," he mumbled and hurried away.

Jen shrugged, wondering what he was up to, and headed toward the storage shed. Plodding along, head bent, at first she didn't notice anyone in the parking lot. Then she saw Mrs. Adams rummaging around in the trunk of her car. Putting down the box with a sigh of relief, Jen walked over.

"Do you need help with something?"

Mrs. Adams shrieked and slammed the trunk shut. "Oh! You scared the daylights out of me!"

9
Coughing
to Death

"Sorry," Jen said. "I didn't mean to sneak up on you. I just thought you might need help getting something out of your trunk."

Mrs. Adams laughed breathlessly, a fluttering hand still pressed against her throat. "Oh, no. I was just trying to rearrange it a bit. I've bought so many souvenirs at the local shops, I wanted to be sure they will all fit in when I leave. Of course," she lowered her voice, "I have every reason to believe I'll be coming back very soon."

"Are you going to get the job?" Jen asked.

Throwing up her hands, Mrs. Adams said, "I can't be positive, but I do have a good feeling about it."

Jen smiled and nodded toward the box of paints. "I guess I'd better get back to work. See you later."

With a cheery wave, Mrs. Adams headed into the B&B.

Jen stored the paint in the shed and found Zeke in the kitchen washing his hands.

"Everyone's back from the interviews," she said. "I just saw Mrs. Adams in the parking lot. She bought a bunch of stuff in town and she's trying to figure out how to fit it all into her trunk. All I saw in there was a toolbox, so she should have plenty of room."

"A toolbox?" Zeke asked, wiping his hands dry. "Why does she have a toolbox in her trunk?"

"What's so strange about that?" Jen asked, turning to wash her hands. "Aunt Bee keeps hers under the sink."

Zeke shrugged. "You're right. I guess all you females are strange."

He laughed. But then, in a sudden burst of pain, he winced. "Oooh, my aching ankle. I don't think I can help you clean the rooms, Jen."

"You're faking it," she protested.

"No, it really, really hurts." He limped over to a chair.

"I'll get you for this! Just wait!" With her brother's laughter ringing in her ears, she gathered up the cleaning supplies and left the kitchen.

Though the guests had just finished up a day of intensive interviews, most were not in their rooms. Instead of following the strict order Zeke had set for when they cleaned, Jen decided to mix up the rooms just for fun.

Dr. Bowles was out for a walk so she went to his room first. As she cleaned, quietly whistling to herself, she sensed that something wasn't right. But she couldn't quite put her finger on what it was. With a shrug, she finished up and moved on to the next room.

It wasn't until Jen was sweeping Mrs. Adams's floor that she realized what had seemed strange about Dr. Bowles's room. His carved box was missing!

Mrs. Adams showed up just as Jen was locking the woman's door. "My goodness, but you do work hard," Mrs. Adams said.

"Just part of living at a B&B," Jen responded. "But I really don't mind." Jen excused herself then and moved down the hall. She lugged her pail through the foyer, where she met Mr. Mitchell heading out for a jog.

"I'm going to clean your room," she called after him. "Is that okay?"

"Go ahead," he said over his shoulder. "Doesn't need much cleaning, though." He closed the front door behind him.

Jen grinned when she peeked into his room. She was the only person she knew who would agree with him. But even for her the mess was a bit extreme.

Leaving the door open, she began sweeping wherever she could set the broom down on the floor. That took about two minutes since not a lot of floor showed between the shoes, magazines, and clothes.

Someone coughed behind her while she was scrubbing the bathroom sink.

Startled, Jen whirled around to come eye to eye with a slightly hunched-over Mrs. Adams. "Oh, it's you," she said with relief, only now realizing how on edge she felt. She was sure she'd be a lot more relaxed when they'd solved this mystery.

Mrs. Adams coughed again, holding a large handkerchief to her mouth. Her face turned brighter than her hair as the coughing continued.

Beginning to feel alarmed, Jen asked, "Are you okay?"

The woman shook her head.

Daggers of alarm shot through Jen. "Did—did someone poison you?"

"No," Mrs. Adams croaked out. "Water."

"You need some water?"

Mrs. Adams nodded vigorously.

Still feeling a bit alarmed, Jen looked at the glass on Mr. Mitchell's sink. It had toothpaste drippings on the side. Ick.

"I'll be right back," Jen said. She ran out of the

room and through the dining room to the kitchen. Jen grabbed a clean glass and filled it with cold water from the tap. She ran back to Mr. Mitchell's room. The room was empty, but she heard coughing coming from down the hall. It wasn't hard to follow the hacking sound to Mrs. Adams's room.

Jen handed her the water.

Her bright red face faded as Mrs. Adams drank nearly half the glass, then gasped for breath. "Oh, thank you, dear." She coughed again and finished the water. "My goodness. Something started to tickle my throat and it simply wouldn't stop. I thought I'd expire!"

"Like the date on a milk carton?" Jen asked, puzzled.

Mrs. Adams laughed. "In a way. To expire in this case means to simply pass away. To die."

Jen shivered. "Well, I'm glad you didn't—uh— expire," she said. Then she laughed as Slinky scooted out from under the bed with Mrs. Adams's handkerchief between her teeth.

"Oh, dear," Mrs. Adams said, looking startled.

Jen picked up the long-haired cat. "Naughty kitty," she said, hugging Slinky. "Sorry about that. Slinky is more curious than most cats."

Mrs. Adams pulled her handkerchief away, then Jen tossed the cat out the door. "If you keep your door closed, she won't bother you."

"I'll remember that. Thank you so much for the water, dear. My glass is full of flowers. You saved my life."

Jen grinned. "Just one of my jobs around here." With that, she hurried back to Mr. Mitchell's room and quickly finished cleaning. It was a nice day, and she'd rather be outside tossing a softball with Stacey.

She worked her way upstairs, dusting the banister as she went. Remembering their plan to inspect the scene of every accident, Jen bent over and examined the carpet at the top of the stairs. She peered at it closely, but there was no bump or tear that could have tripped Mr. Mitchell. Someone *must* have pushed him down the stairs. Either that or he faked it. She sighed. They weren't any closer to solving the mystery.

Ms. Hartlet had left a note on her door not to disturb her. Jen stood outside her door a moment and wondered how someone could have put a snake in the room. The crack under the door didn't seem big enough. The only way was for someone to drop the snake through the ventilation window above the door. The house was so old that it was built with small windows above every door so that even when the doors were closed, a breeze could flow through the rooms. But knowing *how* it was done didn't help solve *who'd* done it.

When she knocked on Mr. Crane's door, no one answered. Jen popped her head in, happy to see that his room looked as tidy as ever—not a scrap of paper out of place. Cleaning it took no time at all.

Lugging the broom, dustpan, and bucket with cleaning solvents out of the room, she locked the door behind her.

"Where is it!" a man's voice bellowed downstairs. "Who took it?"

10

Eavesdropping

Jen dropped everything and nearly flew down the stairs. She knew only one person with a voice that deep.

Sure enough, Dr. Bowles stood in his doorway, his round face purple with anger. "Someone stole my box!"

By now, everyone had gathered except Mr. Mitchell, who was still out running. Even Zeke had hobbled into the foyer to see what was going on.

"Someone stole my box right out of my room. I must find it!"

"Why would someone want to steal it?" Zeke asked Jen quietly.

"Maybe it's an antique and worth a lot of money."

"Or maybe there's something valuable inside it, and that's why he keeps it locked."

Aunt Bee patted the large man's arm. "I'm sure we'll find it," she said soothingly. "We can all look for it right now. What does it look like?"

Dr. Bowles described the size, color, and the dragon design on the box, including the initials carved above the lock.

Mr. Crane said he'd look upstairs, but Zeke heard him go into his room and lock the door. Everyone else spread out to hunt for the missing box.

Jen followed Ms. Hartlet and Mrs. Adams into the dining room. Mrs. Adams said quietly, "I don't know what all the fuss is about. The man is so absent-minded, he probably left it somewhere himself."

As the two women scouted around the dining room, Jen looked through the kitchen, not expecting to find the box. She did find a fresh batch of peanut butter cookies, though, and stopped to quickly refuel her growling stomach.

Meanwhile, Zeke limped into the parlor. Even though he knew Jen thought he was exaggerating about his ankle, it really did throb. Looking for a stolen box didn't sound like much fun.

He sat on the floor to rest for a bit. Woofer lunged over to him, put his paws on Zeke's shoulders, and pushed him over.

"Enough, Woofer," Zeke said with a laugh as the dog licked his ear. But Woofer was too strong to easily push away and too stubborn to stop.

The hot, sloppy tongue tickled, and Zeke rolled on the floor laughing. "Stop it, Woofer!"

Zeke was twisting around, trying to keep his sore ankle out of Woofer's clumsy way, when he spotted something brown and square under the easy chair in the corner. He pushed the dog away and crawled to the chair. He reached under it and pulled out Dr. Bowles's box.

Jen walked into the parlor at that moment. "You found it!" she exclaimed when she saw what he held in his hands. "Where was it?"

"Right under this chair."

"I wonder who hid it there."

"Mr. Crane maybe?" Zeke suggested.

"But why would he do that? It doesn't make any sense."

"Nothing about this case makes sense."

Jen lifted her eyebrows. "Case? That's a box, not a case."

"I was talking about the case we're trying to solve. You know, the mystery of who's causing all these accidents?"

"Oh, right, the case," Jen said, rolling her eyes. "I think you've been reading too many mysteries," she added with a grin. Then she called, "We found it!"

Footsteps thumped toward the room. Dr. Bowles

burst into the parlor. He snatched the box out of Zeke's hands, closely examining the lock.

"Where was it?" the man asked.

Zeke pointed. "Under that chair."

For a second, Dr. Bowles looked surprised. "Oh." With that, he turned and abruptly left the room. A moment later they heard him call, "Thanks."

The twins sat on the sofa with Woofer asleep at their feet. Now that the box had been found, the B&B was quiet again. Too quiet. Jen could feel herself get sleepy. Just as she started to doze off, she heard a voice coming from the foyer. She and Zeke looked at each other.

Jen put a finger to her lips.

Zeke silently mouthed the words, "Mr. Crane."

Nodding, Jen stood and tiptoed toward the parlor door to hear better.

"It's all falling apart," Mr. Crane said. He was obviously talking on the phone that was kept at the front desk. None of the rooms had private phones.

His voice faded out, then she heard, "People suspicious . . ."

Jen took a step closer to hear better. Behind her, Zeke hopped closer, too. He landed on a squeaky board. It screeched like an angry cat. The twins froze. The voice in the foyer stopped abruptly.

A moment later, Mr. Crane said, "I have to go. I love you, too, dear."

The twins heard the phone click down in its cradle. They hustled back to the couch. Sure enough, a second later, Mr. Crane stuck his head into the room. "Do you two always eavesdrop on private calls?" Without waiting for an answer he snapped, "For your information, I was talking to my wife."

Jen and Zeke slouched lower in their seats after Mr. Crane left. "He must think we're a couple of snoops," Jen said.

"I don't think this is what Aunt Bee meant when she said we should make a good impression. If Mr. Crane is our next principal, we're in big trouble!"

"You said it."

"But do you think he really was talking to his wife?" Zeke asked.

"He said *I love you* to someone."

"Maybe that was just a cover-up. Everything else sounded pretty suspicious."

As they sat there thinking, Mr. Mitchell came back from his run. He popped his head into the parlor and said, "Could I get something cold to drink? I just ran ten miles."

Jen jumped up. "Sure. I'll get something from the kitchen."

Mr. Mitchell followed her. She filled a large glass with water. He drank it down in less than thirty seconds. "Whew, that tasted great," he said, wiping sweat off his brow. "Nothing like water to quench your thirst."

Jen opened her mouth to respond when a crash and crackle of breaking glass filled the air!

11

Leave Now
or Else!

Jen's heart raced faster than her legs could carry her down the hall. Mr. Mitchell stayed close at her heels. By the time she'd found the source of the commotion, she was out of breath. The guests were packed just inside the door to Mrs. Adams's room. Jen pushed between bodies to the front of the group so that she could see what was going on. Zeke was already there.

"What happened?" she gasped.

Zeke pointed.

A dumbbell lay on the floor. A piece of paper was taped to it. Shards of glass shimmered all around. With a sinking heart, Jen realized someone had thrown the dumbbell through Mrs. Adams's window.

"It's Mr. Mitchell's," Jen commented to her brother.

He nodded. "Obviously someone threw it."

"But who?"

Mrs. Adams sat on the edge of her bed, her face in her hands. "This is terrible," she wailed. "Just terrible."

Aunt Bee tried to calm her. "Don't worry. I'm sure we'll get to the bottom of this." Then Aunt Bee stepped gingerly over to the weight and plucked the piece of paper off it. She read out loud, "'Leave now or else!'"

Dr. Bowles stepped forward. "Let me see that." Aunt Bee handed him the note and he examined it closely before passing it on to Ms. Hartlet, who handed it to Mr. Crane. Everyone got a good look at the letter except the twins. When the note circled around to Aunt Bee again, she stuffed it into the pocket of her skirt without showing it to Jen and Zeke.

Mrs. Adams couldn't stop crying. "Who would do such a thing?"

Everyone glanced at one another.

"Whose dumbbell is it?" Ms. Hartlet asked.

Mr. Mitchell stepped forward. "It's mine, but I didn't throw it through the window."

"Someone did," Dr. Bowles said. "And if it's your dumbbell . . ." He let his voice trail off.

Mr. Mitchell clenched his fists. "I didn't do it. I was in the kitchen when I heard the window breaking." He turned to Jen. "Isn't that right?"

Jen nodded. "He couldn't have done it."

"When did you notice you were missing a dumbbell?" Mrs. Adams used her large white handkerchief to dab at her eyes. "You must have realized it was gone."

Zeke leaned closer to Jen and whispered, "How could he notice anything in his mess of a room?"

Jen jabbed her brother in the side. "Very funny," she whispered back. But she had to admit Zeke did have a point. How many times had she "lost" something in her room when it was just hidden under a sweatshirt or a pile of books?

"I've had enough of this," Mr. Mitchell said, throwing up his hands. "I'm leaving! I'm sure I would have gotten the position, but no job is worth getting hurt over! This has become ridiculous." With that, he stormed out of the room.

For a moment, no one said anything. Then Aunt Bee cleared her throat. "I'm so sorry this has happened. I don't know how to explain it. Perhaps we should call the police?"

"That seems a bit extreme," Mrs. Adams said, taking a steadying breath. "None of this is going to scare me off, though I wouldn't blame any of you for leaving. Mr. Mitchell has the right idea. I'm just too stubborn to give up."

"Could it really be one of us doing all this?" Ms.

Hartlet asked, nervously sweeping loose strands of hair back into her bun.

Mr. Crane snorted. "Who else could it be? Now, if you'll excuse me, I have to prepare for the last round of interviews." He left without another word.

Dr. Bowles and Ms. Hartlet excused themselves, too.

Aunt Bee patted Mrs. Adams on the shoulder. "Are you sure you'll be all right?" When she nodded, Aunt Bee said, "The twins will clean up the glass, and I'll get the window boarded up right away."

While Jen fetched the vacuum and a box to put the glass in, Zeke gingerly moved the weight out of the way. It was really heavy, and with his sore ankle, it was hard to lug it clear of the broken glass. Mrs. Adams didn't offer to help. She just sniffled from her bed.

After Jen and Zeke had put all the visible pieces of glass into the box, Jen ran a vacuum over the floor to suck up the tiny slivers.

The twins left the room, carrying the dumbbell and the box of glass with them.

"Thank you, dears," Mrs. Adams called after them.

"No problem," Zeke called back before he shut the door.

"We'd better clean up the glass outside the window," Jen suggested.

Zeke shrugged. "I guess we can, but most of the

glass should have fallen inside from the force of the weight smashing through the window."

They left the heavy dumbbell on the check-in desk and exited the B&B. Walking around the perimeter of the house, they stopped outside Mrs. Adams's first-floor window.

"I told you," Jen said triumphantly, pointing to the pieces of glass glimmering in the afternoon sunlight. "Glass can fall the other way, too."

"You just think you're so smart," Zeke teased his twin.

Jen grinned. "I don't *think* it, I *know* it!"

Laughing, they picked up the rest of the glass and added it to the pile already in the box.

"I'll take it to the bins," Jen offered when they were done. She could see that Zeke's ankle was bothering him again.

Zeke flashed her a grateful smile. "Thanks."

Jen watched him limp away, then she carried the box to the recycling bins they kept on the side of the house next to the garbage.

Just as she was rounding the corner of the house, she saw Mr. Mitchell stuff his last bag into his trunk, slam it closed, get in the car, and zoom off without looking back. Jen grinned. What a wimp. He pretended to be so tough, but look at who was the first one to take off. At least she and Zeke hadn't had to help him with all his luggage!

She dumped the glass in the glass bin and put the box in the paper bin. Slinky appeared out of nowhere and pounced at her foot. Jen laughed. Then the cat batted at a piece of red plastic before diving between two of the bins. A second later, the cat tugged on a red-white-and-blue bag that had somehow gotten stuck between the bins. Jen was just about to reach down and help Slinky when she heard a car pull into the driveway behind her. She waved as Detective Wilson pulled up in his silver SUV.

"Did Aunt Bee call you?" Jen asked after he parked.

He nodded as they walked into the B&B together. "Asked me to board up a window. Someone threw a dumbbell through it?"

"Yep." She told him the story. "Look." She pointed to the check-in desk. "Mr. Mitchell didn't take his weight with him. He must have been so upset he forgot."

"Hmmm," Detective Wilson murmured. "I wonder if we can get fingerprints off it."

"Fingerprints? You mean, like, *real* fingerprints?"

Detective Wilson laughed. "Isn't that the only kind? Now, did you or anyone else touch it?" Clasping his hands behind his back, he looked closely at the plastic-covered weight.

Jen thought a moment. "Zeke picked it up, and I put it over here, but I didn't see anyone else touch it."

Detective Wilson nodded. "Great. Then if we find anyone's prints besides yours, Zeke's, and Mr. Mitchell's, we'll have the guilty person!"

12

Dusting for Prints

"Wow, it's that easy?" Jen asked.

"Not necessarily," Detective Wilson admitted. "But it's a good place to start."

"A good place to start what?" Zeke asked, hopping into the foyer.

Detective Wilson's bushy eyebrows pulled together. "What happened to you?"

Zeke waved his hand like it was nothing. Then he told the retired detective about his bike ride to Dead Man's Curve.

"I don't like the sound of this," Detective Wilson said thoughtfully when Zeke was through with his story. "The sooner we find out who's doing this, the better. Let's get started on the fingerprinting."

Jen looked at the dumbbell closely. "So how do we see the fingerprints?"

"You can't see them until you brush special powder over the object. Then, all of a sudden, finger-prints appear all over it," Detective Wilson explained.

"Let's get going," Zeke said. "What kind of dust do we use?"

"That could be a problem," the detective said, scratching his chin. "The police use dust made especially for fingerprinting. It's very fine, and it comes in different colors. It's also made of different chemicals depending on what they want to lift the fingerprint from."

"You mean they use different powders for glass and paper?" Zeke asked.

"Exactly."

"Powder like baby powder?"

"Oh, no," Detective Wilson said. "That isn't fine enough. But we can make our own fingerprinting powder out of charcoal."

"How?" Zeke asked.

"We'd have to grind the charcoal into a very fine dust, right?" Jen asked.

"Right."

"We could use a mortar and pestle," she added. "Aunt Bee keeps one in the kitchen for crushing nuts."

Detective Wilson smiled. "Perfect. We'll also

need a very fluffy brush, some clear tape, and a sheet of white paper."

"I'll get everything," Jen offered.

"We'll meet you in the kitchen."

Jen trotted off and Detective Wilson pulled a large bandanna out of his pocket. Zeke watched as he used the square of red cloth to pick up the dumbbell. "This way we won't contaminate it with my prints," he explained as they moved to the kitchen and waited for Jen to return.

She met them at the kitchen table with her arms full. She'd found a chunk of charcoal from a bonfire outside. Then Jen triumphantly held up the large fluffy brush she had found. "A blush brush!"

"Good thinking," Zeke said. "Where did you find it?"

Jen gulped. "Uh, with Aunt Bee's makeup and stuff. She doesn't ever use it. And it's for a very good cause." *A little charcoal won't hurt the brush, right?* she thought.

She brought the mortar and pestle over to the table, and Zeke proceeded to grind a hunk of the charcoal into a fine dust. Jen leaned over to inspect his work.

"Looking good," she said. Then a sudden tickle in her nose erupted into a sneeze. All the black powder in the mortar exploded into the air. Jen sneezed again.

"Good going," Zeke cried. His hands and arms were covered with charcoal dust.

Detective Wilson laughed. "The dust must be making you sneeze. You'd better stand back a little."

With an extra-heavy sigh just for his sister's benefit, Zeke started to grind another piece of charcoal. This time he finished without anyone sneezing.

Very carefully, using the blush brush, the detective brushed some of the fine powder across the dumbbell.

Zeke held his breath. In a couple of seconds they'd know who was behind all the dangerous accidents.

Sure enough, as Detective Wilson ran the soft brush over the plastic, the fine black powder clung to smudgy fingerprints. Zeke moved in closer, peering at the prints. He knew what fingerprints should look like, and these marks only looked like black blobs.

"Aha!" Detective Wilson exclaimed.

Jen and Zeke leaned in even closer. "What?" they said at the same time.

Detective Wilson explained that most of the blobs were no good, just as Zeke had thought. But on the side of the dumbbell, there was one perfect fingerprint.

He tore off a piece of clear tape and pressed it against the dumbbell, perfectly covering the black print. Then he lifted the tape in one smooth motion. "If you don't do this carefully," Detective Wilson explained, "you'll create lines through the fingerprint that will get in the way when you're trying to identify it." He gently affixed the tape to a piece of white paper.

Once he had finished lifting the first print, he brushed the other side of the weight. They found four more perfect prints. But on closer inspection, they all agreed that two of them looked exactly like the one they'd already lifted. The other two were different, so they lifted them and taped them next to the first one on the white paper. The second two prints were much smaller than the first.

Detective Wilson thoughtfully tapped the blush brush on the side of the table. "I'm afraid these prints aren't going to help us very much after all."

"Why not?" Jen asked.

"The larger prints are all the same, right?"

Jen and Zeke nodded.

"I think we'll find those prints belong to Mr. Mitchell. And these two smaller prints belong to you two. We can fingerprint you to be sure, but I'll bet your aunt Bee's next apple pie on it."

Zeke felt any remaining hope drain out of him.

Jen rushed out of the kitchen and returned holding a glass in a napkin. "Mr. Mitchell used this to drink water. Let's compare prints on this to the prints we already have."

They fingerprinted it and, sure enough, the prints matched exactly. Then the twins fingerprinted each other and found that the smaller prints on the dumbbell were theirs.

Zeke sighed. "Whoever threw this through the window must have worn gloves—"

"Ms. Hartlet had gloves in her room," Jen interrupted excitedly. "And she was acting so nervous before in Mrs. Adams's room!"

"That doesn't mean she's guilty," Detective Wilson reminded the twins. "Somebody could have used a paper towel or cloth. Anything to keep fingerprints off the weight. I'm afraid this was a waste of time."

"Not really," Jen said with a grin. "Now I know how to take fingerprints so I'll know if Zeke borrows any of my CDs without asking."

Zeke smiled. "I'll trick you." He held up his hands and wiggled his fingers. "Gloves!"

Jen laughed. "Criminals are just too smart nowadays."

"Not really," Detective Wilson said. "You'd think they would always wear gloves to avoid leaving fingerprints, but many times, criminals forget to cover their hands."

"Not in this case," Zeke said glumly.

Detective Wilson stood up. "I'd better go board up

that window for your aunt." He winked at them. "She promised me an extra-big slice of pie as payment."

Aunt Bee found the twins wiping up the charcoal dust on the kitchen table a few minutes later. "Is that my blush brush?" she asked, peering closely at the table. "And my mortar and pestle? Why is it all black?"

They explained what they'd done and promised to clean everything.

"I should hope so," she said sternly. "Did it work?"

"The fingerprinting worked, but it didn't point to the culprit," Jen explained.

"Maybe if we had the note," Zeke hinted, "we could analyze the handwriting?"

"I don't think so." Aunt Bee dug through her skirt pocket and her hand came out holding a piece of paper, which she placed on the table in front of the twins.

Zeke and Jen stared at it. It was the threatening note, all right, but Aunt Bee wasn't kidding when she'd said they couldn't analyze the handwriting.

"'Leave now or else!'" Jen read. "The letters are all cut from magazines!"

"Anyone could have done this," Zeke added with a groan.

The twins sagged. "Now what are we supposed to do?"

13
Totally Clueless

"Mr. Mitchell!" Zeke exclaimed.

Jen looked at her brother. "What about him? He's gone. I saw him leave."

"Don't you remember all the magazines in his room?"

"That's right!" Jen stopped and thought a moment. "That doesn't make sense, though. Remember, he was with me in the kitchen when someone threw the dumbbell through Mrs. Adams's window." She shook her head doubtfully. "I don't think it could have been Mr. Mitchell, but I suppose we shouldn't totally rule him out, either."

Zeke picked up the note and stared at it as if that would give him answers. "The magazines Aunt Bee keeps in the parlor for the guests! That's it!" He jumped to his feet. "Ouch! I forgot about my twisted ankle." He hobbled out of the kitchen, through the dining room, and into the parlor. "I was straightening these up earlier, and I noticed some cut pages. Look." He flipped through the most recent issue of *B&B Life*. Several pages were neatly cut or missing altogether.

Jen frowned. "But it could have been anyone, since everyone has access to these. Every time we get a good clue, it just leads us back to the beginning."

They flopped on the couch. Woofer ambled over to them and lay his big, hairy head between them.

Jen laughed and tousled the hair in front of Woofer's eyes. "So what now?"

"I guess we should make suspect sheets to try to figure out what's going on."

The twins went to the lighthouse tower for privacy and settled on Jen's bed. They wrote out suspect sheets for each guest.

Mystic Lighthouse

Suspect Sheet

Name: Mrs. Adams

Motive: wants job

Clues: 1. She was almost run off the cliff by a red car. Who did it?

2. SHE DIDN'T WANT TO CALL THE COPS.

3. Why was she snooping around in Dr. Bowles's room?

4. IS SHE THE ONE WHO HID HIS BOX IN THE PARLOR? SHE COULD HAVE SEEN IT WHEN SHE WAS SNOOPING IN HIS ROOM, BUT WHY WOULD SHE WANT IT?

5. DUMBBELL WAS THROWN THROUGH HER WINDOW WITH THE NOTE ATTACHED.

Mystic Lighthouse

Suspect Sheet

Name: Dr. Bowles

Motive: wants job

Clues: 1. Not afraid of snakes and has a snake ring. Could he have put the snake in Ms. Hartlet's room?

2. Out late and opened side door to sneak snake in?

3. Did he really find Mr. Crane's briefcase or did he hide it in the bushes himself?

4. What's in his locked box? And why are there strange initials on the box?

5. Too jolly to be believed?

Mystic Lighthouse

Suspect Sheet

Name: Mr. Crane

Motive: wants job

Clues: 1. He was the one to point out only ONE of them would get the job.

2. WHO STOLE HIS BRIEFCASE?

3. Very suspicious phone conversations.

4. Acts nervous, like he might be up to something. Very mean to everyone.

5. HIS ROOM IS UPSTAIRS. COULD HE HAVE PUSHED MR. MITCHELL DOWN THE STAIRS?

6. Was he really talking to his wife about "everyone suspicious" or did he fake the "I love you, too, dear," just to throw us off the track?

Mystic Lighthouse

Suspect Sheet

Name: Ms. Hartlet

Motive: wants job

Clues: 1. Acting very nervous.

2. Her room is upstairs. Could she have pushed Mr. Mitchell down the stairs?

3. She had gloves, so she could have taken the dumbbell without leaving fingerprints. But how did she get into Mr. Mitchell's room?

4. What was in the letter that she got? Why did she tear it up? And why did the part Jen found say, "Do whatever it takes to get the job"? Did that mean hurting or even killing the others to get them out of the way?

Mystic Lighthouse

Suspect Sheet

Name: Mr. Mitchell

Motive: wants job

Clues: 1. Has a dented car!

2. DID HE REALLY GET PUSHED DOWN THE STAIRS? OR DID HE TRIP? OR DID HE FAKE IT?

3. AND WHY WAS HE UPSTAIRS? HE SAID HE WAS LOOKING FOR HIS STOPWATCH. BUT WAS HE JUST SNOOPING AROUND? OR WAS HE UP THERE TO PUT THE SNAKE IN MS. HARTLET'S ROOM AND SHE JUST DIDN'T SEE IT UNTIL THE NEXT DAY?

4. It was his dumbbell that was thrown through Mrs. Adams's window.

5. LEFT THE SCENE OF ALL THE CRIMES. BUT WHY, IF HE WANTED THE JOB SO MUCH?

Jen snorted with disgust. "This is impossible. We'll never figure out what's going on."

"I know what you mean." Zeke's shoulders slumped. "We must be missing a really important clue."

"What, though?"

"I don't know. But if we could find something, I bet everything else would fall into place."

They sat silently for a minute, then Jen said slowly, "We have to go back to the beginning again—back to Dead Man's Curve."

Zeke gulped. His ankle hardly even twinged anymore, but the thought of what could have happened to him put a rock in his throat. "Aunt Bee won't like it," he said, knowing this wouldn't stop his twin.

"We'll just say we're going to the Quick Stop Mart."

"Okay," Zeke reluctantly agreed. Even though he knew Aunt Bee wouldn't like it if she found out, he knew this was the only way to get to the bottom of things.

Fifteen minutes later, he found himself riding around the first bend of Dead Man's Curve. He rode so far off the side of the road that he almost ran head-first into a pine tree.

"Watch where you're going!" Jen shouted.

They jumped off their bikes and left them in the

ditch before running across the road. With her hands on her hips, Jen looked around. "That's weird," she said.

"What?"

"Where are the skid marks?"

"I noticed that, too," Zeke admitted. "I didn't think it was important, though. Mrs. Adams probably exaggerated her accident. After all, it was just a little fender bender."

"It didn't even dent her fender. It just broke her taillight," Jen pointed out.

Zeke frowned. "You know, I never did find any pieces of the taillight."

"What do you mean?" Jen asked, scouting around.

"We saw the broken taillight on her car, right?"

Jen nodded.

"I didn't find any pieces of it when I was here last time, and you don't see any now, right?"

Jen shook her head.

All of a sudden they heard the roar of an engine and tires screeching as a car barreled around the tight bend of Dead Man's Curve.

"Watch out!" Zeke shouted.

Note to Reader

Have you figured out who is behind all the accidents? It's clear that one of the candidates for the principal's job wants their competition to be scared away. But who?

If you review this case carefully, you'll discover important clues that Jen and Zeke have missed along the way.

Take your time. Carefully review your suspect sheets. When you think you have a solution, read the last chapter to find out if Jen and Zeke can put all the pieces together to solve *The Mystery of Dead Man's Curve*.

Good luck!

Solution
Another
Mystery Solved!

Zeke grabbed Jen's arm and yanked her back to the shoulder of the road near the guardrail. The car raced past on the other side of the road, squealing as it rounded the last turn of Dead Man's Curve. Even as it disappeared from sight, the roar of the motor lingered.

"What did you do that for?" Jen demanded, rubbing her arm where Zeke had grabbed her.

Zeke glared at her. "Only to save your life. Aren't you going to thank me? That maniac driver was trying to kill me again."

Jen's eyes widened. "You mean that was the same car that tried to hit you?"

"I'm positive," Zeke said, nodding.

"But I thought you didn't get a good look at it. How can you be sure?"

"The sound of the motor. There must be a major

hole in that car's muffler to make it so loud. It was definitely the same one."

Jen laughed. She couldn't help it.

He scowled at her. "See if I try to save your life again," he said. When Jen didn't stop laughing, he asked her what was so funny.

"I'll tell you later. I promise," she added as his scowl deepened. "Let's just say that part of this mystery is solved. But that doesn't help with the missing taillight." She looked around at her feet.

"It's as if the accident never happened," Zeke mused out loud.

The twins froze as Zeke's comment sank in. Jen snapped her fingers. "Mrs. Adams's toolbox!"

Zeke knew exactly what his sister was thinking. "A hammer."

"Mrs. Adams broke her own taillight. She faked the accident!" Jen exclaimed.

"She must have pulled over somewhere to smash her own car."

"I've got it," Jen called over her shoulder as she ran across the road and hopped on her bike. "Come on!"

Zeke followed Jen at top speed to the Quick Stop Mart. He winced with each downward pedal on his sore ankle, but he didn't slow down. At the store, they raced inside and Jen headed right for the check-out counter where Stacey's brother, Brian, was waiting on a customer. When the customer left, Jen said, "Hi, Brian. Were you working last Sunday?"

Brian looked at the ceiling a second, then nodded. "Yep. What's up?"

"Do you remember waiting on a really tall lady with bright orange hair?"

"Frizzy, like clown hair?" Brian asked right away.

"Yes!"

"Sure, I remember her. She was a little strange. She asked me for a bag, but when I said I couldn't give one out without a purchase, she bought something just so she could have one."

"A toothbrush and toothpaste?" Zeke asked.

"Something like that," Brian agreed.

The twins looked at each other, their blue eyes flashing with excitement.

Jen started with, "Remember Slinky and how . . ."

". . . she was playing with that piece of red plastic," Zeke finished for her.

"Mrs. Adams put the taillight in the bag and threw it away, but Slinky found it."

"Mrs. Adams faked the whole accident."

"If we can find those pieces of plastic, we can prove it!"

"Hey, what's going on?" Brian interrupted.

"Oh, nothing," Jen said, trying to sound casual even though she was jumping with excitement inside. "By the way," she went on, changing the subject, "were you almost late for work today?"

Brian tried to hush her. "Keep it down. The manager said if I'm late one more time, I'm fired. And I need the money to fix my muffler."

Zeke's mouth dropped open and Jen laughed.

"Do you drive an old green car?" Zeke demanded.

Brian grinned. "Yep. Isn't it great?"

"Great?" Zeke burst out. "You almost killed me. Twice!"

"What are you talking about?"

Jen quickly explained how his squealing tires and broken muffler had startled Zeke at Dead Man's Curve.

"You really thought I'd run you off the cliff?" Brian asked Zeke, looking sheepish. "I admit I was going a little over the speed limit, but my tires are low on air, which is why they squeal. And you know about the muffler now. I'm really sorry I scared you."

"I wasn't scared," Zeke said, straightening his shoulders. "Just—uh—concerned."

"We have to go now," Jen said quickly. She started out of the convenience store, making sure Zeke was right behind her.

When they finally made it back to the B&B, they rode right to the garbage bins. Sure enough, there was Slinky, sitting on a red-white-and-blue-striped bag from the Quick Stop Mart as though she were waiting for them. Jen remembered how Slinky had been playing with it earlier, but she hadn't made the connection. Now she pulled the bag out from under the cat and looked into it. She passed it to Zeke without a word.

Zeke peered into the bag at all the smashed pieces of taillight. There was a slight tear in the side where a couple of pieces of plastic must have slipped out for Slinky to play with. "But why? Why would she fake it?"

Jen snapped her fingers. "All the accidents, of course. She was trying to scare everyone away from the job interviews. But if nothing happened to her, it would look suspicious."

"So she made sure the first accident happened to her," Zeke continued. "That way, when things started happening to the other candidates, she wouldn't look guilty."

"That must be why her dent isn't rusty, but Mr. Mitchell's was. His was from an old accident."

"This is all fitting together now," Zeke said.

After a moment of thought, Jen said, "Mrs. Adams had a coughing fit and asked me to get her a glass of water."

"So?"

"I was cleaning Mr. Mitchell's room at the time! And when I came back to give her the water, she was in her room again. That's when she stole the dumbbell!"

"But what about her fingerprints?"

"She had a handkerchief! I thought it was because she was coughing, but it was probably what she used to pick up the weight."

"Perfect!" Zeke exclaimed. "And remember how I said there shouldn't be that much glass outside her window because the weight was thrown *in* and not *out*?"

Jen nodded. "And you were so surprised when I was right. But I should have been wrong! She must have used the weight, or something else heavy, to break the window from inside her room. Then she broke off pieces of the window and dropped the glass in her room so it wouldn't look suspicious."

"She sure is sneaky."

"But how do we prove it?" Jen asked.

"Fingerprints."

"But there weren't any incriminating prints on the weight," Jen protested.

Zeke pulled the note out of his pocket. "How about this?"

They went inside and set up a fingerprinting lab at the kitchen table, then dusted the note for prints.

It was covered with them.

Zeke groaned. "I just remembered that the note was passed around the room. *Everyone* touched it."

Jen started to say something, but the charcoal dust tickled her nose. Even though she tried to stop it, a giant sneeze erupted, blowing dust everywhere. On her second sneeze, the note fluttered.

"Did you see that?" Jen asked, trying not to sneeze again.

Zeke was brushing the black dust off his shirt. "See what?" he asked grumpily.

"Watch." Jen blew lightly on the note. The letter *E* at the end of ELSE flapped up. Most of the letters were glued securely, but this *E*, the largest letter in the note, was only tacked down at the top.

Realization crashed into Zeke's brain. "Finger-prints!"

Very carefully, they dusted the underside of the *E*. Sure enough, one single print showed up. Zeke lifted it very carefully with a strip of tape and affixed the tape to a clean piece of white paper.

Jen inspected the print. "Are you sure you lifted this smoothly?"

"Of course," Zeke said.

"Then what's this line through the fingertip?" She passed the paper to him for a closer look.

"It looks like a cut or a scar."

"Can you tell which finger it is?"

Zeke shook his head. "It looks smaller than a thumb and bigger than a pinky. But other than that, I have no idea."

Jen picked up a scrap of paper and pretended to cut it out, put a dab of glue on the back, and place it down as though she were going to stick it to another piece of paper. "Did you see that?" she asked her brother when she was done.

"Yes, but what's your point?"

Jen showed him her pointer finger. "It's this finger. And . . ." She held up her hand to stop her brother from interrupting. "And Mrs. Adams has a scar on that exact finger from when she cut herself on the day she arrived. She just showed me yesterday how well it was healing. There's a thin scar across her finger just like this fingerprint!"

"What are you two doing?" Detective Wilson asked, leaning over the table.

The twins jumped.

"We figured out which guest is guilty of causing all the accidents," Zeke announced.

Rushing and interrupting each other, the twins told Detective Wilson the entire story, including all the clues they'd missed at first.

"She must be the one," Jen finished. "But now what do we do?"

Detective Wilson nodded thoughtfully. "You two have done enough. In fact, you've done an excellent job. I'll go talk to her. Stay put. There's no telling how angry she'll get, and she could get dangerous."

Jen and Zeke longed to go with him, but one stern look from under his bushy eyebrows kept them from arguing.

When Detective Wilson didn't return immediately, the twins got restless. First they cleaned up their mess, then they settled in the parlor, straining their ears to hear anything from down the hall.

It seemed as if everyone else knew something was going on. Pretty soon all the guests and even Aunt Bee were sitting in the parlor. At last the retired detective returned.

"She's gone," he said, shaking his head. "She admitted to absolutely everything. You kids hit it right on the nose."

"So she faked her accident," Jen said.

"And did everything else, too. She even pretended to hate snakes and she put the snake in Ms. Hartlet's room."

Ms. Hartlet shuddered. "What a dreadful woman."

Jen and Zeke continued to explain how they figured out Mrs. Adams was the guilty one.

"But," Zeke admitted, "we are still a little confused about some of the things we wrote down on our suspect sheets." He turned to Dr. Bowles. "For example, the first night you were here, you came in late. What were you doing?"

Dr. Bowles smiled sheepishly. "I tend to be a bit forgetful, in case you hadn't noticed. I couldn't remember if I'd turned off my headlights when I'd arrived, so I went outside to look. And before you even ask, I have to admit that I took my pillbox downstairs to sort through my medicine, and I forgot that I left it under my chair. I'm sorry I accused someone of stealing it."

"Your pillbox?" Jen said. "You mean your dragon-carved box is full of pills?"

"I take medication for high blood pressure, high cholesterol, allergies, and migraine headaches. I keep the box locked because my grandkids visit, and I don't want them getting into my pills."

"You have a lot wrong with you!" Jen exclaimed without thinking.

Dr. Bowles laughed. "I sure do. It's all from stress. Now I try to keep a positive outlook. It seems the happier I am, the fewer ailments I have. But I have to admit, it's not easy to be jolly all the time."

Zeke laughed. "That certainly explains a lot. But whose initials are on the box?"

"Those are my mother's. It was her pillbox long ago."

Jen turned to Ms. Hartlet.

Ms. Hartlet opened her eyes wide and said, "Surely I wasn't a suspect, too?"

"We did wonder about that letter you got," Jen admitted. "I found a piece of it that said you should get the job no matter what."

Ms. Hartlet laughed. "Oh, that was from my twenty-year-old nephew. He's always bullying me into trying something new. He thought I might purposely not try hard on the interviews. He thinks I should move up in my career, but he also thinks I'm too set in my ways. Too chicken, is how he puts it. He was just urging me to try my hardest to get the job."

Jen laughed. "Well, what about the gloves in your room?"

Ms. Hartlet looked confused as to why the gloves would make her look guilty.

"It's too warm out for gloves," Jen explained, "and if you're wearing gloves, you don't leave fingerprints. So I thought—"

"Those are my lucky gloves," Ms. Hartlet interrupted, laughing. "They belonged to my grandmother.

I bring them to all important events. Kind of like a lucky coin or a rabbit's foot."

Jen groaned. "Boy, anything can look suspicious!"

"Which is why I was a suspect, too, I suppose?" Mr. Crane asked dryly.

"We didn't mean to eavesdrop," Jen said, crossing her fingers behind her back.

"As I already told you," Mr. Crane snapped, "I was talking to my wife."

Jen and Zeke looked at each other and shrugged. They knew it wouldn't do any good to mention all the suspicious things they had heard him say. And anyway, they'd already found the guilty person.

Just then the phone rang. The call was for Ms. Hartlet, and she went to the front desk to talk.

Aunt Bee sighed. "I'm so relieved all this is cleared up. I was afraid we had a poltergeist at work in the B&B."

"It would be cool to have a ghost," Jen said.

"Cool until you came face-to-ghostly-face with it," Zeke teased.

Ms. Hartlet returned, a stunned look on her face.

Aunt Bee jumped to her feet. "What's wrong?"

Shaking her head, Ms. Hartlet said, "Nothing. I— I got the job! The superintendent of schools said they didn't need to do any more interviews because the hiring committee had already agreed that I should be offered the position." She looked apologetically at Mr. Crane and Dr. Bowles. "I'm so sorry."

Dr. Bowles laughed. "Sorry? Don't be silly. I'm sure you'll make a wonderful principal here in Mystic. To tell you the truth, I'm not sure my heart could take all the excitement around here."

Someone in the corner started to laugh. It was not a familiar sound.

Jen gasped. Mr. Crane was laughing so hard that tears were spilling from his eyes. At first she thought he was hysterical with disappointment.

"I'll be fine," Mr. Crane said through his laughter and tears. "I am just so relieved!"

"Relieved?" everyone repeated in unison.

Mr. Crane stretched his arms above his head, looking more relaxed than Jen thought he ever could have. He began to explain. "I love my job. I'm a principal at a small middle school where we have wonderful students. But my wife wanted to move and thought I should have a more prominent position. I love her dearly, but my wife can be a bit pushy." He laughed again.

Jen could hardly believe how sweet he looked when he smiled.

He turned to the twins. "I really was talking to my

wife when you *accidentally* overheard me. I kept telling her how nice the other candidates were and how I'd never be able to compete at the interviews. It all must have sounded rather sinister to you two."

Jen and Zeke grinned. "It sure did!"

"I'm sorry I've been rather, uh, cranky. I don't do well at all under extreme pressure."

"Oh," Ms. Hartlet said, still beaming, "I should probably tell you all what else they said on the phone. The superintendent asked to speak to Mrs. Adams. When I told him she had left, he said the strangest thing. He said that Mrs. Adams had forged some of her letters of recommendation and, in fact, had been fired from her last job! That must be why she was so desperate to scare everyone else away from the job. She knew she didn't have any chance of getting it otherwise."

Slinky slipped into the room then, her fluffy tail waving proudly. Instead of climbing on Woofer, who was sleeping at the twins' feet, she crawled under the sofa and backed out with a cord between her teeth.

Jen squatted down and took the string from her and pulled. The rest of the object appeared. "Mr. Mitchell's stopwatch!"

Zeke laughed. "Another mystery solved!"

The Mystery
of the Missing Tiger

For Sheryl, John, Matt, and Josh

Contents

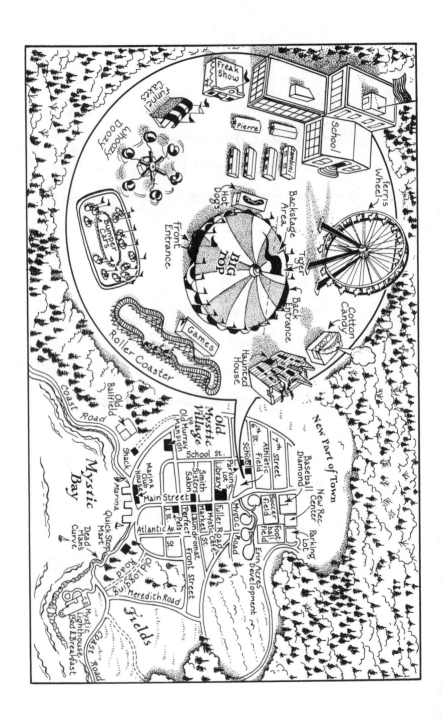

Disaster Under the Big Top

"This is so cool!" Jen exclaimed, nudging her best friend Stacey in the ribs. She'd never been to a circus before and didn't know where to look first. Fresh Maine air wafted through the open flaps of the red-and-white-striped big-top tent. Sitting in the fifth row with her twin brother, Zeke, and their best friends Stacey and Tommy, Jen had a great view of the dusty ring in the center of the tent.

Zeke checked his watch. The show wouldn't start for another ten minutes. "Good thing we got here early," he commented as more and more laughing people crowded into the big top. He saw groups of kids from school and waved. Little kids ran in, their faces buried in big pink puffs of cotton candy. Their parents hurried in after them.

Jen nodded. "We lucked out getting the circus

right here at Mystic Middle School. I'll bet all the high school kids are bummed that they had to rush over after school from the other side of town!"

Stacey stood up to stretch out her leg.

"What's wrong?" Jen asked.

Stacey grimaced and leaned down to massage her plump calf. Her short, curly blond hair fell forward. "I think I pulled a muscle at yesterday's game when I jumped up to block that ball."

"It was a great save," Jen said. "We won because of you." Now their soccer team, the Mystic Monsters, would go on to the playoffs.

Stacey sat down and tenderly rubbed her leg. "I just hope I can play by next week. I don't want to miss the first game at the new field." Yesterday's game was the last that would be played at the old recreational field. From now on, all the teams would get to play at the brand-new ballfield. The awesome new clubhouse even had showers and an indoor pool. The old field only had a beat-up old shack that barely protected the equipment from rain.

"Just think, we've lost our last ball to the Atlantic Ocean," Jen added, remembering how she had kicked the soccer ball over the fence yesterday, sending it rolling over the cliff and down to the ocean below.

"And now we'll be able to hear Coach Riley's

instructions!" Stacey said, her light blue eyes sparkling.

Jen laughed. The only thing louder than Coach Riley's voice was the sound of the ocean crashing right near the old field. You couldn't hear anything on days when the ocean was whipped into a frenzy by a coming storm or an especially strong wind. It was about time the Mystic recreation department built a new field and clubhouse.

Zeke leaned forward and pointed toward the ring. "Look, they're gonna start."

The crowd cheered as three clowns tumbled into the ring, pushing each other and then somersaulting out of each other's way.

"That one looks like a kid," Jen said, pointing to the shortest clown. He wore a blue-and-green polka-dotted clown suit, and his bright green hair stuck out in tufts all over his head. A huge smile was painted on his face, and his nose was covered by a red-and-blue ball.

The boy clown jumped forward onto his hands and walked around the entire ring while the other clowns playfully somersaulted and cartwheeled in his way. When he stood up again, the audience clapped wildly.

Five jugglers ran into the ring, their bright yellow-and-black costumes making them look like buzzing bees. They were tossing fluorescent pink balls around and around and back and forth at a dizzying rate.

"And I thought *I* was good with a soccer ball," Jen said with a sigh of admiration. She could keep a ball in the air for a long time, bouncing it with her head, knees, and ankles, but these jugglers were truly amazing. "I guess I can't join the circus."

Zeke laughed. "Don't feel bad," he said. "Aunt Bee would never let you go, anyway. Who would help me clean the bed and breakfast?"

Jen smiled. They had been living with Aunt Bee ever since their parents' death when the twins were just two years old. Aunt Bee, their grandmother's sister, had become like a parent to them. Living in the Mystic Lighthouse B&B was perfect. The twins got to live in the remodeled lighthouse tower, and they ate very well, since Aunt Bee was the best cook in town.

Suddenly, the crowd hushed. A tall, bald man with an enormous, glossy black handlebar mustache marched into the spotlight.

"Welcome! Welcome! WELCOME!" he said as he turned in a full circle. "I am Pierre the Magnificent, and I welcome you to my circus—the Most Amazing Show on Earth!" He lowered his voice. "Or at least in Maine," he added in a loud whisper.

The crowd laughed.

"We have a fabulous show for you this afternoon.

Sights you have never imagined! Animals that behave like humans! The Great Zambinis, who fly through the air with the greatest of ease!" He held up his hands to stop the applause. "But you must all come back on Friday night . . ." He paused. "To see Terra the tiger trainer in action with our new, our very own, very special, and very rare Siberian tiger!"

A golden-haired woman wearing a black leotard and sparkling tights ran into the ring. She was as tall as Pierre and very thin. When she bowed in their direction, Jen noticed she had catlike eyes. Terra clawed the air with her bloodred fingernails, and her mouth pulled back into a snarl.

"She looks even more fierce than a tiger," Stacey whispered to Jen.

Jen nodded. She wouldn't want to mess with the Siberian tiger . . . or its trainer!

As soon as Terra took her bows and ran out of the ring, Pierre announced the first act. "Please welcome Patti's Prancing Ponies!"

Everyone cheered as six adorable, ginger-colored ponies circled the ring, tossing the bells on their fluffy manes in time to the music. Jen didn't know where the next hour went. One after another, varied acts impressed and amused the crowd. After the ponies came trumpeting elephants, ostriches that flipped large green balls back and forth over a net, and then acrobats who made a human tower that was ten men high. Between the acts, the clowns entertained the audience with their silliness. There were at least seven different clowns, and two of them were obviously kids around Jen and Zeke's age.

Jen looked around at the audience. The crowd was enthralled—laughing and clapping and pointing to things all over the ring. About five rows behind her, Jen noticed Mrs. Watson—Jen and Zeke's science teacher at Mystic Middle School—with her plastic pocketbook in her lap. Everyone knew Mrs. Watson was a strict vegetarian, and she used no animal products. She had once told Jen that even her hair dye was all natural and had never been tested on animals—which is why the color didn't always come out as planned. Right now it looked sort of greenish.

Jen waved, trying to get her teacher's attention. But Mrs. Watson sat stiffly, staring down into the ring with her face set as still as stone into a fierce frown. This was unusual—Mrs. Watson was good at telling jokes, and she liked to have a good time. She made science class fun by creating all kinds of neat experiments. Jen gave up trying to get her teacher's attention, but wondered why Mrs. Watson was the only person in the audience who wasn't having fun.

A drumroll sounded. Pierre the Magnificent moved to the center of the ring and held out his hands for quiet. When he finally got it, he announced, "And now the finale . . . the Greeeeeaaat Zambini Family!"

Spotlights focused on two poles at opposite sides of the ring that reached nearly to the top of the tent. A man and a teenage boy climbed up the pole on one side of the ring, while a woman and a girl who looked slightly younger than the boy climbed up on the other.

"I'm getting dizzy just watching them. I hope no one falls," Stacey whispered.

"They're trained for this," Jen said, craning her neck to watch the trapeze artists. She barely noticed that a safety net was spread across the ring in case one of them did fall. The Zambinis arranged themselves on the tiny platforms at the top of each pole. The father and mother simultaneously untied trapezes that had been secured near the platforms with ropes. The man handed the tiny swing—really just a bar suspended between two long ropes—to the teenage boy by his side, while the woman passed her trapeze over to the girl.

The drumroll stopped abruptly and was replaced by gentle, melodic music over the loudspeakers. The girl and the boy swung back and forth. The boy hung upside down and hooked his legs over the bar. Jen gasped as the girl let go of her bar in mid-swing, twirled through the air, and caught the boy's outstretched arms. It looked almost effortless, but Jen couldn't breathe again until each of them was standing on a platform, bowing to the wildly excited audience below them.

Mr. Zambini grabbed a different swing and swung out over the center of the ring. He locked his legs and ankles over the bar and pumped his arms so he went higher and higher with each swing.

The next thing happened so fast that Zeke wasn't sure he was seeing correctly. Then he heard a loud cry from everyone around him. One of Mr. Zambini's ropes had broken and he was plunging to the ground!

Searching for Clues

Zeke jumped to his feet and watched, horrified, as Mr. Zambini fell into the net below.

"Oh no!" Jen gasped, trying to see over the heads of everyone standing up in front of her. "Is he hurt?"

Pierre rushed into the ring, along with several of the clowns. They helped Mr. Zambini off the net and onto his feet. The crowd erupted into applause when Mr. Zambini waved to the fans and limped out of the ring. Pierre remained behind to announce that tonight's circus would be canceled, but reminded everyone to return for Friday's show. "In the meantime, enjoy the rides outside!"

"Mr. Zambini could have been killed if that net hadn't been there," Tommy said after Pierre hurried out of the ring. He ran a hand over his buzzed brown hair. "I can't believe he didn't break an arm or leg."

"Or his head," Zeke added. "That was a really lucky fall."

Jen tightened her lips. "Or unlucky, depending on how you look at it."

The twins glanced at each other. They had seen enough strange occurrences before to wonder if this accident had anything to do with luck at all.

"Let's go see if Mr. Zambini is okay," Zeke suggested casually.

Tommy lifted his eyebrows at his friend. "You can't fool me, Dale," he said, using the twins' last name. "You're snooping. Well, I hate to disappoint you, but this was obviously just an accident. No mystery here."

Zeke shrugged. "You're probably right." Then he grinned. "But it can't hurt to look, right?"

Tommy rolled his brown eyes. "I'm not wasting my time looking for nonexistent clues. I'm hungry. Anyone want to go eat?"

The twins shook their heads, and Stacey said, "I have to get a story about the Zambini family for the school paper. This will definitely make the front page." She started down the bleachers. "I'll find you when I'm done," she called over her shoulder.

With a wave, Tommy joined the crowd heading

out of the tent. Jen and Zeke hopped over the seats to the ground level and headed backstage.

The area behind the ring was chaotic with performers milling around in their glitzy costumes, mixing with several people who looked as out of place as Jen and Zeke felt.

Jen caught sight of Stacey trying to push through the crowd surrounding the Zambinis, her notebook and pen in hand.

Zeke pulled Jen back as she started to follow her friend. "Let's wait till the crowd dies down a bit."

Jen nodded. They backed out of the way until they came up against some metal bars. Jen turned around to see what had stopped their backward progress and almost screamed. Instead, she caught her breath and grabbed Zeke's arm.

Zeke felt the alarm in Jen's grip and turned to look behind him. They were face-to-face with the huge head of the white Siberian tiger! The tiger was absolutely enormous.

"Good kitty," he mumbled, taking a hasty step away. "Good kitty!"

The tiger opened its mouth as if to yawn, but suddenly a tremendous roar bellowed out from deep in its chest. Jen stumbled back in shock. The tiger licked its lips, blinked twice, then took three turns around the cage. Its muscles rippled gracefully with each step. Jen knew it could take her head off with one bite if given the chance. She shivered. Thank goodness it was behind steel bars!

Terra rushed over, her green eyes flashing. "Lady," she crooned. "Hush, Lady." She stuck her arm between the bars and scratched the tiger's massive head.

Jen and Zeke hurried away. When they were a safe distance from the cage, Zeke felt calmer. "I think I'd be a pretty good tiger trainer," he told his sister.

Jen lifted one eyebrow, something she had been practicing for months now. "Oh, really? Maybe after your knees stopped shaking."

Pierre's loud voice cut through the noise of the crowd. The twins turned to look. "Get out of here," the circus owner barked at a woman, his bald head wrinkled and red with anger.

Jen thought she recognized the odd, green cast to the woman's hair. Sure enough, when she turned, Jen saw it was their science teacher, Mrs. Watson. What was she doing back here, and why was Pierre so upset about it? Before Jen had a chance to find out, Mrs. Watson ducked out of sight.

Zeke pulled Jen behind another cage, grateful to see it wasn't filled with anything kid-eating, just two chattering monkeys. "Don't let Pierre see you," he warned. "We don't want to get kicked out of here before we have a chance to look around."

They watched Pierre head toward the tiger cage, where he confronted Terra about something. The twins were too far away to hear their conversation clearly over all the commotion backstage. Zeke edged forward, trying to stay partially hidden at the same time.

"You have to trust me," Terra said, a sharp edge to her voice. Her greenish cat eyes narrowed. "Trust me."

Pierre tugged nervously on one side of his mustache. "But everything depends on you. You have to pull this off, especially after what happened tonight, or we'll be ruined."

Terra scowled, looking fiercer than ever. "Don't worry, I've got it all planned. You'll get your money."

"I'd better!" With that, Pierre hurried away.

"What was that all about?" Jen asked Zeke when they had wormed their way through the crowd to avoid being seen by Pierre.

Zeke shrugged. "It sure didn't sound good, that's all I know."

Now that the crowd was thinning, Stacey had finally gotten through to the trapeze artists. Jen and Zeke heard Stacey's high, clear voice over the sounds of all the rides and amusements outside.

"Mr. Zambini, are you all right?" Stacey asked.

Jen and Zeke craned their necks to watch their friend in action.

Mr. Zambini nodded. "No problem," he said. He had a slightly foreign accent. "My leg is a little sore, but I'll go to the doctor tomorrow and everything will be fine."

Stacey scribbled something on her pad. Then she looked up again. "What happened to the rope?"

Mr. Zambini looked rueful. "I did not check it as I should have. It must have been frayed from overuse. I am just thankful that my dear wife and children were not injured." He hugged his wife to his side.

Stacey continued her questions. "How do you feel about Terra and her tiger taking over the spotlight of the show?"

Mr. Zambini's face turned red and for a split second contorted into an angry mask. But he regained control of himself and smiled thinly. "That is also no problem. The Great Zambinis are just that—great! Nothing can be greater! No more questions."

By now, the worried onlookers had left, and the backstage area was almost deserted. A couple of clowns were still chatting off to the side, and Zeke noticed a portly man standing in the shadows. He couldn't be sure, but it looked as if the man was wearing a fancy suit with a vest and watch chain over his rounded belly. When he raised his right hand to shoo away a bug, Zeke saw a flash of glittering diamonds on his pinky.

"Come on," Jen said, distracting Zeke for a second. When he looked back, the stranger was gone.

Zeke headed toward the exit, managing to pass as close to the Zambini family as possible.

"When William hears about this, he'll be worried," Mrs. Zambini fretted, her eyes red and her long, thin nose sniffling back tears. The two children had their mother's nose and their father's pointy chin.

Mr. Zambini put a hand on his wife's shoulder. "Call him, then, if it makes you feel better." He lowered his voice. "And tell him not to worry about the tuition money."

Jen poked Zeke in the back and urged him along faster. As they shuffled toward the exit, they caught sight of Mrs. Watson, who seemed to be trying to linger in the shadows without being seen while edging toward the tiger cage.

"What's she doing?" Jen asked Zeke.

"Let's go ask her," he suggested.

But at that moment, Mrs. Watson looked over at the twins. She frowned and disappeared behind several cartons of corn kernels that were obviously being stored there for the popcorn machine.

"Why is she avoiding us?" Jen said, about to head after their science teacher.

Zeke held her back and motioned behind them with his head. "Maybe she was looking at him, not us."

Jen turned and gulped. Pierre was headed right for them, a dark scowl on his face.

3

Nothing but Air!

The twins didn't wait for Pierre to reach them;
they scurried out of sight as quickly as possible, ignoring Pierre's shouts commanding them to stop. Out of
breath, they finally edged out of the big top. The sun
had set, and the lights from the rides and games
sparkled and shimmered.

"There's Mrs. Watson," Jen said, pointing. "Let's
see what she was doing."

They followed her, trying to catch up, but the
crowds kept getting in the way. When they reached a
large circle of people watching an informal clown act
near the cotton candy booth, they lost her for good.

"We'll have to ask her tomorrow in class," Jen said.
"She was probably nosing around like we were." Then
she smiled. "Or maybe she wants to join the circus."

Zeke laughed, but shook his head. "I don't think

so. Anyway, we haven't figured out what happened to Mr. Zambini's rope yet. I don't believe it was an accident."

"Let's go back into the ring," Jen suggested. "Maybe there's a clue there."

They sneaked around to the front entrance of the big top, afraid Pierre would jump out at them any second and demand to know what they were doing.

"The coast is clear," Zeke whispered.

The twins ducked into the big tent. The deserted ring looked a bit spooky now that the spotlight was off and the other lights had been dimmed. High above them, the trapeze towers disappeared into the darkness.

The large blue flap covering the entrance to the backstage area fluttered occasionally, but no one came through as Zeke and Jen quietly made their way into the ring. The sawdust covering the ground muffled their footsteps. They went around the ring in opposite directions, scouting around for clues. Jen found a tassel from one of the prancing ponies, and one of the jugglers' pink balls, but that was all.

"Find anything?" Jen whispered when she and Zeke met up on the other side of the ring.

Zeke shook his head. "Something that might have been elephant droppings," he whispered with a slight scowl, "but that's it. Seems like this is a waste of time. We may as well enjoy a couple of rides before Aunt Bee picks us up."

Jen shook her head, looking up. "I have an idea." Zeke followed her over to one of the trapeze towers. "What are you doing?"

Jen put her hand on the first rung of the ladder-like steps that ran right up the pole. "If I go up there, I might be able to inspect the rope."

"Are you crazy?" Zeke exclaimed, forgetting to keep his voice down. Just looking up the pole made him dizzy. "Just because you can climb a tree like a monkey doesn't mean you can climb this. You could get killed."

Jen didn't answer. The next thing Zeke knew, she was at least ten feet above him and climbing steadily. His hands were slick with sweat, watching her nervously from below. He wanted to shout, "Get down from there!" but he was afraid that any loud noise would startle her. There was no net on this side of the trapeze tower.

Jen tried not to think about how far away the ground was. "Hand, foot, hand, foot," she kept repeating. She kept her eyes straight ahead. If she looked down, she knew she would be doomed.

Luckily she was in great condition from all the

hours spent on the soccer and softball fields. But her nerves were eating away at her energy. She was worried that if she didn't make it to the top soon, her legs might give way.

Just as she was tempted to give up and head back down, her hand hit the platform. She carefully scrambled over the edge and rested for a long moment on her hands and knees.

"Are you okay?" Zeke's voice floated up to her.

She took a deep breath and peeked over the edge of the narrow platform. "I'm fine," she replied. Zeke was just a dark shadow about a million miles below her. She closed her eyes. *Don't look down*, she reminded herself.

Trying to calm her nerves, she slowly stood up. All the trapeze ropes had been gathered and tied together and attached to the pole. Keeping one hand on the small handle jutting out from the post, she leaned forward and grabbed the ropes, trying to tug them closer to her. They swung a little, but not close enough for her to examine them. She realized she'd have to let go of her handhold.

Was the post swaying, or was that her imagination? *Get a grip*, she told herself firmly. She edged closer to the ropes, reluctantly letting go of the pole. Gingerly, she grabbed hold of the broken rope and

examined it closely. This was no accident—the rope
had been cut!

"Hey!" someone shouted from below.

Jen jumped in alarm. Her foot slipped. She lunged
wildly for the ropes, the post, anything to grab onto,
but all she felt was air rushing past all around her!

Sabotage

Jen tried to scream, but the sound got stuck in her throat. She tumbled through the air, falling . . . falling. . . . Instinctively she twisted and curled into a ball just in time. She landed on the net, which felt like a very large trampoline. When she stopped bouncing, she scrambled to the edge of the net, leaned over and grabbed the underside, then flipped over and off of it, landing gracefully on solid ground.

Zeke grabbed her in a bear hug. "I thought you were a pancake."

Jen hugged him back. "So did I," she admitted with a shaky laugh. "Who was the jerk who yelled?"

"I was," said a boy clown wearing a polka-dotted suit, with a big smile still painted on his face. But Jen could see that under his makeup, he was frowning.

"What do you think you were doing up there?" the boy demanded.

Jen felt her spine stiffen. "I was just checking something out. Who are you, anyway?"

The clown boy narrowed his eyes. "Checking something out?" he asked doubtfully. "Not trying to cut the ropes?"

"No way!" Jen exclaimed.

"We'd never do that," Zeke said before his twin could say something she'd regret later. She had a bad habit of putting her foot in her mouth. "We just want to know what's going on."

The clown relaxed and he grinned. "Sorry about that," he apologized. "I guess I'm kind of upset about Mr. Zambini's accident." The clown turned to Jen. "I'm really sorry for scaring you. I thought maybe someone was up to no good. I'm glad you're okay. Oh, and my name's Mitchell, by the way."

The twins introduced themselves, both wondering if Mitchell could be trusted.

"I thought maybe the rope was cut or something because some strange stuff has been happening lately," Mitchell admitted. "When I saw you up there, the first thing that ran through my head was that the jerk who did it was back. I'm really sorry."

Jen waved away his apology. "Don't worry about it. You were just trying to protect the circus." She looked at Zeke and he nodded. "And you were right about the vandalism. Before I fell I saw the rope. Someone cut through it with a knife. Only a little edge of it was frayed. Also, I noticed some masking tape on the rope, as though whoever had cut the rope left a little still attached, then covered their work with the tape to disguise it."

"So none of the Zambinis would have noticed it when they got up there," Zeke added.

Jen nodded. "Exactly. And they were so involved with the audience, they obviously wouldn't notice it later, either. Not until it was too late."

Mitchell shuddered, his big blue-and-red nose wobbling on his face. "Who would want to ruin our show like that?"

"That's exactly what we want to find out," Zeke answered. "Do you know anyone who would want to hurt the Zambinis?"

"But it's not only the Zambinis," Mitchell said quickly. With crossed eyes, he pointed to his nose. "Look at this. It used to be red, but right before the show someone splattered blue paint over all the clown noses in the dressing room."

"That's not exactly as bad as cutting a trapeze

rope," Jen pointed out.

Mitchell frowned. "It may not seem like much to you, but clowns are very particular about their noses. And costumes have disappeared. Also, the other day the ostrich trainer found a metal spike in the ostrich cage. Luckily none of the birds got hurt."

"Someone is definitely trying to damage the circus," Zeke said thoughtfully. "We didn't find any clues here, but maybe we should check out the dressing room. You said stuff has been happening there, too."

"Sure," Mitchell said, leading the way. "I'll show you. I've worked and traveled with the circus all my life. My parents are two of the jugglers. I don't know what we'd do if Pierre closed down the show."

"Maybe we'll be able to help," Jen said. She didn't tell Mitchell that they had successfully solved other mysteries. She didn't want to raise his hopes, just in case.

The clowns' dressing room was a long trailer that had been painted on the outside with giant, smiling clown faces. Inside, it smelled like greasepaint, sweat, and dirty socks. All of the clowns were still in costume out on the grounds. Mitchell told them it was part of their job to entertain the crowds after a show until closing time. When the rides stopped at eleven P.M., there would be a mad rush in here with all seven clowns trying to remove their makeup at the same time. He waved his hands as he spoke, pointing out the dressing area and the brightly lit, mirrored make-up tables.

"What do you do about school?" Zeke asked.

Mitchell wrinkled his nose. "Don't worry, I can't get out of that. Pierre hired a teacher who travels with us and teaches all the kids. There are fourteen of us who live with the circus."

"Neat," Jen exclaimed.

Mitchell shrugged. "I guess it's pretty cool. But sometimes I wouldn't mind staying in one place longer than a week or a weekend. I'd like to live in a house for a month and see what it feels like."

"I guess that isn't so neat, after all," Jen said, changing her mind. She couldn't imagine not living at the B&B with Zeke and Aunt Bee.

"Anyway," Zeke interrupted, "where do you keep your noses?"

Mitchell pointed out the counter. Whoever had vandalized the noses had gotten blue paint on the countertop as well. "And we keep our costumes on this rack." He pointed. "We each have about four or five costumes because we sweat a lot in them and it's not good to wear the same one night after night." He swung a few hangers out to show them. "These are mine. I was the first to notice that one was missing. When we searched, we found several were gone. Everyone else thought the missing costumes were getting washed. But when we asked Jack, the man in charge of all the laundry, he said that he didn't have them."

"Who would want clown outfits?" Jen asked, amazed. Then she hastily added to Mitchell, "No offense."

Mitchell grinned. "You mean you wouldn't want to wear this to school?" He held out a red, white, and blue puffy one-piece suit and tapped his oversized shoe in pretend annoyance.

"Uh, it's very patriotic," Jen laughed. "Honestly, you wouldn't catch me dead in that—unless, of course, I was a clown."

Mitchell laughed, too. "Sometimes I do wear this to school . . . clown school!"

The twins warmed up to Mitchell, who straightened the rack of clothes. "These are old costumes," he said, pointing to several shoes and outfits at the end of the rack. "We wear out our costumes pretty quickly from jumping and rolling around, but sometimes it's hard to get rid of a favorite."

Jen nodded. "I have T-shirts like that. I can't bear to get rid of them, but Aunt Bee won't let me wear them anymore."

"None of this helps solve the mystery of who is trying to sabotage the circus," Zeke pointed out. "If we don't figure this out soon, the next accident could be even worse!"

A New Suspect

The next morning, Jen stuffed her books into her backpack. After the circus the night before, Aunt Bee had picked them up and driven them home. Jen and Zeke had spent the rest of the evening doing homework.

"Why can't teachers cancel homework when there's something this exciting going on in Mystic?" she asked Slinky, her Maine coon cat. Slinky just yawned.

"Thanks a lot," Jen said with a laugh. "You're sure a big help."

"Ready?" Zeke asked, peeking in her door.

Jen hoisted her backpack over her shoulder and followed her brother down to the kitchen where they each grabbed a homemade cranberry-almond muffin.

"We're riding our bikes to school," Jen reminded Aunt Bee.

Aunt Bee nodded, sipping her cinnamon tea. Her long gray hair wasn't in its usual braid, but hung loosely down her back. "Have a great day," she said with a smile.

Zeke jumped up and exclaimed, "Of course we will. Today's Friday!"

"Shhh," Aunt Bee hissed. "Mr. Richards, the guest who checked in yesterday, is on the parlor phone and he asked not to be disturbed. He was quite upset that the guest rooms didn't have phones in them."

"He doesn't have a cell phone?"

Aunt Bee shrugged. "Apparently not. But take a look at his car as you leave," she said with a twinkle in her blue eyes. "Just tiptoe out."

Zeke motioned for Jen to follow him. They could have left through the back door in the kitchen, but he wanted to get a glimpse of Mr. Richards.

They crept by the parlor, but all they saw was Mr. Richards's slicked-back, glossy black hair and his back.

"That's right," Mr. Richards said. "Buy all five of them. Can never have too many bucks."

The twins moved on. "He must be a banker," Jen whispered.

They went outside and around the side of the

B&B. Zeke whistled in amazement. "He's got lots of bucks all right," he said, pointing to a small green sports car in the parking lot. "That must have cost him a fortune."

"It looks like an insect," Jen remarked, mystified. "What is it?"

"It's a Lamborghini, and it's worth hundreds of thousands of dollars!"

The twins raced down the B&B's long driveway. Then they pedaled on the side of the road that led into town. A few cars sped by them. They had ridden for about five minutes when Jen spotted a large, white truck with a black triangle painted on the side that had pulled over to the side of the road. The truck was very clean. The front hood was up and a man was peering at the engine.

Zeke braked to a stop. "Need any help?" he asked.

The man looked up and smiled, showing off a gold front tooth. "I sure do, kid. Know anything about truck engines?"

Zeke shook his head. "I don't, but my friend's uncle does. He owns a garage down the road. We're going right by there and could tell him you need help."

The stranger nodded and glanced at his watch. "That would be great, kid. I really appreciate it. I'm already late."

Zeke smiled. "No problem."

Jen waved to the man as they headed off. As soon as they got to the garage owned by Tommy's uncle, they pulled in and Zeke relayed the message as promised.

Tommy's uncle, Burt, was a gruff man who wore oil-stained coveralls. He thanked them with a nod of his balding head. Jen knew he didn't like kids hanging around the garage, and she urged Zeke away as fast as she could. She knew that even though Tommy loved his uncle, he didn't get in Burt's way, either.

At last they pedaled onto the school grounds. The circus was already bustling with workers feeding animals, and jugglers in normal clothes practicing their moves. Zeke noticed that one clown was already in costume and walking with a slight limp. He saw that the tiger cage was completely covered by a gold cloth with tassels on the edges. He wondered if Mitchell was in school with his circus friends and the teacher Pierre had hired.

The bike rack stood near the front entrance of the school. Zeke parked his bike, not bothering to lock it up. Detective Wilson, a great friend and a retired police detective, had told them that in all the years he worked on the Mystic police force, not even one bicycle had ever been stolen.

Jen parked her bike next to Zeke's. "I wonder what's going on over there," she said, looking toward a cluster of trailers where circus workers had gathered.

"Someone's mad about something," Zeke said, hearing an angry voice. "Let's check it out before the bell rings."

They hurried through the gathering crowd until they stood in front of one of the trailers. From the outside, everything looked fine. But Pierre stood in the doorway, shouting angrily, his mustache jerking up and down with each word. Jen stared at the circus owner. He was covered with splotches of blue paint.

"It's ruined," Pierre shouted. "Everything in my trailer is ruined! Blue paint everywhere! When I catch the vandal, he will pay!"

Jen learned from the bearded woman standing next to her that Pierre had left his trailer early that morning, but when he'd gone back to get something, he'd found the destruction. "So many things are going wrong," the woman murmured, shaking her head.

Not able to help herself, Jen blurted out, "Is your beard real?"

The woman took a step forward. "Of course it is. Wanna pull it?"

"Uh, no thanks." With that, Jen tugged Zeke

aside and told him what the woman had said about the paint in the trailer. "It's definitely part of the mystery," Jen said. "And her beard is real. I asked her."

Zeke rolled his eyes. When would she learn to keep her mouth shut? "At least this wasn't a dangerous accident," Zeke said in reference to the vandalism. "But it sure made Pierre mad." Then he cocked his head to one side and Jen could practically see his sensitive ears perk up. "Oops, there's the bell. We'd better get to homeroom."

They rushed into the building, then split up to head for their different homerooms. Jen hustled and made it to her seat just as the late bell shrilled.

"Where were you?" Stacey asked, leaning toward her. "You weren't on the bus."

"Bikes," Jen said, catching her breath.

The morning announcements came over the loudspeaker; Jen sorted through her books, only half listening as a student talked about next week's lunch menu, the boy's baseball team, and the math team championships. As soon as the announcements ended, Jen stood up, ready to head to first period, but then the principal's voice clicked on.

"One more announcement," she said. "As a special treat, today will be a half-day for students and teachers. Classes will last only twenty minutes each and no lunch will be served. Have fun at the circus this afternoon!"

A cheer erupted in homeroom. Jen looked at Stacey, her mouth in a silent O. "I should tell Aunt Bee it's only a half-day. She knows we're staying after school for the rides, but I should let her know school's getting out early."

On the way to first period, she stopped in the office and borrowed the phone, but the B&B line was busy. It was busy after first period, too. And after second, and third, and fourth. Finally, at eleven o'clock, she got through.

"Who's been on the phone?" Jen exclaimed. "I've been calling you forever!"

Aunt Bee sighed. "It was Mr. Richards. He must have talked to every country on this planet at least twice."

Jen shook her head. "Jeez, if I spent that much time on the phone, you'd have it disconnected."

Aunt Bee laughed. "You've got that right. Now what's so urgent?"

Jen told her aunt about the shortened day, and Aunt Bee asked if they had enough money to buy lunch and still go on all the rides.

"Don't worry, I've got twenty bucks," Jen said, using Mr. Richards's term. She hung up and ran to science class.

Mrs. Watson nodded to her when Jen entered. Stacey had already told her that Jen was trying to call her aunt.

"As I was saying," Mrs. Watson continued, "it is horrible the way they have those poor circus animals locked up and trained to do those silly tricks."

"But they're fun to watch," someone piped up.

Mrs. Watson ran her fingers through her oddly colored hair. Today it had a bit of an orange tinge to it. "It's not fun, it's . . . it's agonizing."

None of the students said anything.

"Especially that poor Siberian tiger, trapped in a cage like that. It's supposed to be a wild animal. It should be free. In fact, I'd do anything to put it back into its own environment. Anything!"

Jen glanced back at her brother, who sat two rows behind her. They raised their dark eyebrows at each other. It wasn't unusual for one of them to know what the other was thinking—it was a twin thing, they'd decided long ago.

Anything? they both thought.

Escape!

When the bell rang at 12:16, everyone cheered. Jen and Stacey met Zeke and Tommy, and they made their way toward the rides and games along with every other middle schooler.

"Sheesh," Stacey grumbled, shaking her blond curls. "Are there enough people here?"

"Let's try the Ferris wheel," Jen suggested. "The line isn't very long."

Before they knew it, Jen and Stacey were sitting on a swaying bench, heading up into the big, blue sky. At first the ride kept stopping and starting as the other passengers got off and on. Finally, it smoothed out.

"Yikes," Stacey said, gripping the bar across her lap. "I didn't know this went so high."

Jen laughed. "But look at the view." They gazed in all directions. Mystic Village spread out at their feet.

Beyond the buildings they could see the fields and the dark forest. To the east they followed Main Street down to the Mystic Marina and Mystic Bay. The Atlantic looked calm and sparkly in the sunlight.

"Hey, there's the B&B," Jen said, pointing toward the lighthouse.

"And there's the old ballfield," Stacey said, nodding south. "It looks so lonely and deserted."

Jen looked around for the new town field and recreation center, pointing it out when she spotted it.

By the time the ride had stopped, the girls had found all the major landmarks. They got off the Ferris wheel before the boys, so they waited for Zeke and Tommy to join them.

"That was cool," Tommy said. "We could see everything."

But Zeke didn't want to stand around talking. "Come on," he said. "Something's wrong."

Jen looked around. "Where?"

"The big top," Zeke called over his shoulder, already heading in that direction. "I saw it from the Ferris wheel."

Jen raced after her brother, Stacey and Tommy close at her heels.

When they entered the backstage area, Jen gulped. The gold covering had been pulled off the tiger cage, and the cage was empty!

"Where's the tiger?" Tommy asked, a nervous tremor in his voice.

"Lady is gone!" Terra said, as though she'd heard Tommy's question. She stood with a group of policemen near the cage. "But how did she get out?"

One of the officers said, "Someone must have stolen her."

"But that's impossible," Terra insisted, narrowing her cat eyes. "I checked on her very early this morning and I'm sure I locked the cage. No one could have gotten in there."

The policeman shrugged. "Does anyone else have the keys?"

"No. . . ." Terra bit her lip. "Well, actually, I misplaced my keys yesterday."

"Then how did you get in the cage this morning?"

"I have a spare set," Terra admitted.

"Someone probably stole your keys," the officer said grimly.

Terra shook her head in disbelief. "But who would want to steal Lady?"

At that moment Pierre charged up to the group. He took one look at the empty tiger cage and exploded. "Where's my star? Where's my tiger?"

A policeman tried to calm Pierre down. "Don't

worry. We'll find the cat. There aren't too many places to hide a tiger in Mystic."

Pierre fumed. He whirled on Terra, gripped her arm and yanked her aside. "This is all your fault," he hissed under his breath.

Zeke wondered if anyone else could hear them. He strained to hear the rest.

"If you don't find that cat, you won't have a job here or anywhere else. I'll make sure of it!"

Terra, who had looked upset before, now narrowed her eyes at Pierre and pulled her arm free. *She looks like Slinky when Slinky is mad,* Jen thought. Stacey and Tommy seemed to be more interested in watching the policemen as they talked into their radios to the rest of the force, who were out looking for Lady.

"You said I could trust you," Pierre went on. "Is this part of your plan? *Now* where will the money come from?"

Terra said something too soft to hear.

Pierre glared at the tiger trainer. "I'd better!" He let go of Terra and looked around. "Zambini. I need the Zambinis. They're all I've got left now. Where are they?" When Mr. Zambini didn't come forward, Pierre looked even angrier.

Finally, a voice called out, "I think my father is at the doctor's getting his leg checked." The girl who stepped forward was Mr. Zambini's daughter, the youngest of the trapeze artists.

"When will he be back?" Pierre demanded, tugging on his mustache.

The girl shrugged. "You said we weren't performing tonight because Terra and Lady were doing an extra-long show for the grand opening of their act."

Pierre stamped his foot. "Disaster!" he shouted, flinging his hands into the air and looking at the sky. "All of this is a disaster!" He marched away without looking back.

A Clue in Blue

Stacey rushed off after Pierre, digging her notebook out of her bag at the same time. "I'm going to try to interview him," she shouted over her shoulder.

"Good luck," Tommy muttered. "I'd rather face a starving tiger than Pierre. Talking about starving, I'm really hungry. Food anyone?"

Jen and Zeke glanced at each other then shook their heads. "Not yet," Zeke said. "But you go eat. We'll find you later."

Tommy shrugged. "It's *your* stomachs." He jogged away toward a sign that read HOT DOGS, SOFT DRINKS, COTTON CANDY, FRIED BREAD.

"Or your stomachache," Jen added to herself. She liked junk food as much as the next person, but not if there was any chance of going on a fast ride after eating it.

A nearby policeman reported to Terra, "So far there's absolutely no sign of the tiger. No one's seen him—"

"Her," Terra corrected.

"Her, or heard her growl or anything. We have all of our staff on patrol, working overtime and extra duty. Don't worry, we'll find Lady. Now, if you don't mind coming down to the station with us, we'd like to fill out a report."

Terra looked nervous for a second, then she gave a small smile and agreed.

By now the crowd had dispersed. Jen and Zeke waited until no one was near the cage, then stepped cautiously inside it.

"I wonder who stole Terra's keys?" Jen asked.

Zeke frowned. "Do you think Terra really lost her keys, or was that just a cover-up? Remember how she told Pierre he would get the money last night? I wonder what that's all about?"

Jen scanned the inside of the cage, looking for clues. "It sure doesn't make her sound completely innocent. But then again, what money is Pierre talking about? If I wanted money from someone, I wouldn't go around yelling at her."

"Maybe it was just an act on Pierre's part," Zeke suggested. He squatted down to look more closely at the straw covering the bottom of the cage. "Jen! Come here!" he exclaimed, trying to keep his voice down.

Jen hurried over and bent low to look. "Blue paint! It's the same color as the clown noses."

"And the same color as the paint inside of Pierre's trailer," Zeke added. "It's definitely the same person behind all of this."

Jen tipped her head sideways. "Brush a little of that straw away."

Zeke brushed the straw away.

"Now brush that away over there," Jen continued. When Zeke did, they both gasped.

Zeke stood up for a better view. "Is that what I think it is?" he asked.

"If you're thinking it looks like the outline of a huge footprint, then you're thinking what I'm thinking."

Zeke nodded. "So either a giant did this, or someone else who wears big shoes."

"The clowns!"

"Exactly. Let's go find Mitchell."

The twins hurried through the fairgrounds to the trailer covered with clown faces. They knocked on the door and Mitchell opened it, already in costume.

"Hi, you guys," he said. He didn't look too happy.

"Is this a bad time?" Jen asked.

Mitchell shook his head. "Did you hear what happened to Lady?"

The twins nodded.

"Everyone's afraid that without his new star, Pierre will shut down the circus. We've been struggling for a

while, but Pierre was hoping the tiger would bring in new crowds."

Jen looked at Zeke. *So that explained the money he wanted. Or did it?*

Mitchell let them into the trailer. "He's actually just canceled tonight's performance because he can't find Mr. Zambini. His daughter said he's at the doctor's office. I guess he hurt his leg pretty bad when he fell last night." He slumped onto one of the dressing room chairs. "We're doomed."

"Not yet," Zeke said. "If Jen and I find the tiger, the circus will be okay, right?"

Mitchell looked back and forth at them. "Of course. But what can you two do?" he asked, waving his hands when he talked.

Jen grinned. "You mean, what *can't* we do!"

Mitchell seemed to catch on to their hopeful mood. "Can you walk around the ring on your hands?"

Jen's grin faded. "You got me on that one."

Laughing, Mitchell said, "Don't feel bad. It took lots of years and a whole bunch of knocks on the head to get the hang of it." Then he sobered. "But seriously, how do you think you'll find the tiger when the police haven't even found it yet?"

"We've already uncovered a clue that they missed," Zeke said. "We found a blue footprint in the straw that the police didn't see. We'll find out whose it was."

Mitchell scrunched his eyebrows together and waved his hand around. "How does that help?"

"The footprint was huge," Jen elaborated. "Like a clown's shoe. And the blue is the same color that was painted on your noses."

"So one of the clowns is trying to ruin the circus?" Mitchell asked. "I can't believe it."

"If we can find the shoe with blue paint on it, we'll know who is sabotaging everything and has the tiger," Jen said, already looking toward the lineup of clown shoes.

Mitchell jumped to his feet. The three of them turned over every pair of shoes.

"Here it is," Zeke crowed, holding up a large yellow shoe.

"That's weird," Mitchell said. As he shook his head, his green clown hair bounced back and forth.

"Weird?" Jen repeated. "Why?"

"No one wears those shoes anymore. It's like those costumes I showed you yesterday. Worn out, but not ready for the garbage. Those shoes used to belong to Petey, and he doesn't even work with this circus anymore."

Zeke frowned. "You're sure you haven't seen any

of the clowns wearing these shoes?"

"I'm sure." Mitchell's face fell. "So much for the clue."

"We may not know exactly who the person is," Jen said, trying to sound cheerful, "but we know it's someone who was wearing those clown shoes."

"I figure that the person first sabotaged Pierre's trailer and got paint on his—"

"Or her," Jen butted in.

"Shoe," Zeke continued, "then hurried to the tiger cage and stole Lady while everyone was distracted by Pierre's problem." He motioned to Jen. "We went over to Pierre's trailer before school, too, to see what had happened, remember? Someone could have been stealing the tiger and no one would have noticed."

Mitchell nodded thoughtfully. "It sure makes sense. So we have to be on the lookout for a clown who's not really a clown."

"Exactly," Jen agreed, realizing that this task sounded nearly impossible. But she refused to give up. Just then her stomach growled loudly. "Well, we missed lunch, and now it's almost dinnertime. We'd better hurry home or Aunt Bee will think we were eaten by the stolen tiger."

The twins said good-bye to Mitchell, retrieved their bikes, and headed home.

"Burt must have picked up that guy's broken-down truck," Zeke commented as they rode closer to the B&B.

"Yup, I noticed it at his garage when we passed it."

They pedaled on, panting heavily as they headed up the long hill to the B&B. The light was fading, and the sun lit up the top of the lighthouse tower. The rest of the B&B sat in shadows.

"Who's that?" Jen huffed, trying to talk and pedal uphill at the same time.

Zeke looked up, too out of breath to answer. Two figures were talking by the side door of the B&B. He couldn't tell who they were.

As they neared the door, Jen peered through the gathering dusk, trying to make out their faces. Something just didn't look right about them, as though they were trying to stay hidden. Just then one of the figures looked up and saw Jen and Zeke approaching. Jen felt certain it was a man. He slipped inside the B&B, leaving the other person alone.

The lone figure flashed them a quick grin as he hurried away on foot, heading down the driveway Jen and Zeke had just come up.

"That was the truck driver from this morning," Jen said when she'd caught her breath.

"Are you sure?" Zeke asked. He thought it was too

dark to be able to make out the guy's face.

"I'm positive," Jen said firmly. "I saw the flash of his gold tooth."

Zeke shook his head as he parked his bike. "What would the truck driver have to do with any of the guests at the B&B?" he wondered out loud.

"I don't know," Jen said, putting down her kick-stand. "But they looked pretty suspicious."

The Perfect Plan

The twins hurried inside, hoping to catch a glimpse of the mysterious stranger, but when they got to the front foyer, a group of bird-watchers who were staying at the B&B were on their way out to dinner. It was impossible to tell who might have been outside a second ago.

Disappointed, they searched for Aunt Bee and found her in the parlor talking to a well-dressed man with shiny black hair. They recognized him from that morning as Mr. Richards. She beamed at them as they walked in.

"Children, this is Mr. Richards, one of our guests."

Mr. Richards stood up to shake hands with the twins. Zeke stared hard at the man. He'd seen Mr. Richards at the circus last night after Mr. Zambini's accident—the man in the fancy suit. Zeke checked out his pinky. Sure enough, Mr. Richards wore a diamond pinky ring that was in the shape of a pyramid.

"Good evening," Mr. Richards said pleasantly, patting his round stomach.

Jen almost felt like she was supposed to bow to this elegantly dressed man. She could tell his clothes were expensive. He sat down again and smiled.

"Mr. Richards was just telling me about fascinating places," Aunt Bee said. "He's traveled all over the world."

Jen noticed the man's briefcase at his feet for the first time. It was covered with travel stickers. It didn't exactly look like something a well-dressed businessman would carry around, but maybe he was eccentric. She peered closely at the stickers.

"You've been to all those places?" she asked. "South America," she read out loud, "Hawaii, the Amazon, Siberia, the Everglades, Africa." The rest of the stickers were partially covered or too small to read from a distance. "I've always wanted to go on a safari in Africa."

The man chuckled. "I've been on at least a dozen safaris there."

Jen was genuinely impressed. "Wow."

Zeke frowned. He couldn't imagine what this man

might be doing with a gold-toothed truck driver. But surely none of the bird-watchers had been talking to the truck driver. Zeke looked up as another man walked into the parlor.

"Is your room comfortable?" Aunt Bee asked the tall man.

Zeke was surprised to see Pierre the Magnificent.

"It's fine," Pierre grumbled. "Too many flowers for my taste," he added with a scowl as he saw the twins.

Jen hid a laugh. Her aunt was used to cranky guests and never got upset no matter how rude they were. "Well, your trailer will be cleaned in no time, and you'll be able to go back to it," said Aunt Bee soothingly.

"Just another added cost," he mumbled. "Had to cancel tonight's show. Do you know how much money I'm losing? Lots. Lots and lots," he stressed. "And now with Lady missing." He shook his head in disgust. "The star of our show gone." Suddenly, he brightened a little. "But thank goodness for the Big Top Insurance Company."

Jen and Zeke looked at each other.

"I'm hitting the hay," Pierre continued. "Circus life starts before the sun is up. G'night." Abruptly he turned away and stomped out of the parlor.

Aunt Bee shrugged. "The poor man is not having a very good time of it. I hope everything works out for him."

Mr. Richards nodded in agreement.

The twins excused themselves and Aunt Bee told them dinner would be ready in about a half hour. They headed up to Jen's room to talk. Each of the twins had a bedroom and a bathroom in the lighthouse tower. Aunt Bee's husband, Uncle Cliff, had renovated it, creating Jen's room on the second floor and Zeke's on the third. A spiral staircase ran from the lighthouse museum on the first floor, past the bedrooms, all the way up to the light itself. Unfortunately, Uncle Cliff died just before the grand opening two years ago, so he never got to see how successful the B&B would become.

Jen loved her partially round room. She had covered her walls with posters of sporting events and soccer stars, as well as a few cat pictures. Jen flopped on her bed, pulling Slinky close to her, and Zeke sat on the beanbag chair near the window.

"So who was talking to the truck driver?" Zeke asked once they were settled.

"I don't know, but I'll bet it was either Mr. Richards or Pierre."

Zeke nodded. "That makes sense, because I don't

think it was any of the bird-watchers. But what does his truck have to do with either of those men?"

"I can't figure that out," Jen admitted. "But if we're going to help the doomed circus in any way, we have to find out." She grinned. "And I have the perfect plan."

Zeke groaned.

~✓~

Early Saturday morning, Jen tapped on Zeke's door. "Ready?" she asked when he opened it.

He yawned. "I guess so." He glanced at his clock. It was after seven, but it felt a lot earlier.

"I told Aunt Bee we'd be leaving early to go to the circus," Jen said. "She said she didn't need help with the breakfast buffet today."

They coasted down the hill on their bikes. The morning mist was cool and smelled like the ocean. Waves crashing against the cliffs sounded muffled, and early gulls were out looking for a bite to eat.

They pedaled silently. Not a single car passed them. At last they rounded the corner where Tommy's uncle's garage sat. It was still dark enough that the outside security lights were on. But as they watched, the lights flickered off automatically one by one.

They parked their bikes on a side street, then

crept silently back to the garage. They had to finish what they were going to do before Burt officially opened the garage at eight.

"There it is," Jen whispered, pointing to the white truck in the mist.

Zeke nodded. They headed for the truck. Jen climbed onto the step by the driver's door and tried the handle. The door was locked. She jumped down while Zeke tried the other side.

"Rats," Jen said when they met at the rear of the truck. "How can we check it out if we can't get in?"

"Didn't you figure the truck would be locked?" Zeke asked.

Jen glared at him. "No. I didn't."

Zeke shook his head. "I should have known this wasn't the perfect plan." Just as the words were out of his mouth, he heard a creaking noise. He turned to find Jen slowly lifting the back door of the truck.

She grinned at him. "They didn't lock the back! Part of my plan, you know."

"Yeah, right."

Whether it was part of the plan or not, they were able to slide under the rolling door. The inside of the truck was dark.

"Can you see anything?" Jen asked.

Zeke squinted. "Not really. What's this all over the floor?"

He heard some rustling, then Jen said, "I think it's straw or hay."

"Look over here," Zeke said. In the shadowed light, they could make out two large, empty plastic bowls. "What are these for?"

Jen peered at the bowls then ran a piece of straw between her fingers. "I'll bet this truck is for the tiger."

Zeke was about to protest, but the more he thought about it, the more perfect it sounded. "That's right, because we saw it the morning the tiger was stolen."

"But it broke down," Jen continued. "So it wasn't there to take the tiger away."

"Then the tiger must still be in Mystic somewhere."

"But where? Whoever stole it couldn't have taken it too far away. They could have used one of the circus vans to take it somewhere, but those vans would be too small to take Lady very far. I know I wouldn't want a frightened tiger sitting in my backseat."

"Shhhh," Zeke suddenly hissed.

Jen heard voices. She recognized the deep voice of Burt, Tommy's uncle.

"I told you," Burt said, somewhere close by, "the truck will get done when it gets done."

"But I need it *now*."

"It's not ready *now*," Burt said.

The other man sighed in frustration. "When, then?"

"Come back at five-thirty today."

"That late?"

"If you keep wasting my time," Burt growled, "it won't be ready till Monday. I'm closed tomorrow."

"It had better be ready by five-thirty," the man threatened. "Or else!"

9

Out of Control

The voices faded away as Burt opened up his office. "Let's get out of here," Jen said.

The twins slipped under the truck door and quietly lowered it. Crouching, they hustled across the parking lot, dodging behind cars and trucks that were waiting to be repaired. Out of breath, they ran around the corner and jumped on their bikes. They didn't slow down until they were on Main Street. Delicious smells were wafting out of the Mystic Café.

"Let's get something to eat," Jen suggested. "It's too early to go to the circus, anyway."

Zeke agreed eagerly. Aunt Bee might be the best cook in town, but the Mystic Café was known for its honey buns, and Aunt Bee didn't even try to compete with them.

Inside the café, the twins sat in a window booth

and ordered fresh orange juice, a double order of honey buns for Zeke, and a toasted sesame bagel with veggie cream cheese for Jen.

While they waited for their order, they talked, keeping their voices down. The café filled up every morning, and they didn't want to be overheard.

Jen leaned forward, her elbows on the table. "So, if the truck is finished at five-thirty, and if it really is to transport the tiger, we're running out of time." She glanced at her watch. It was barely eight.

Zeke nodded. "We have to solve this case—*fast.*"

"We know who the truck driver is, but even if we tell the police our suspicions, they're not going to be able to arrest him without proof."

"That's right. We need to find evidence."

"What we need to find is Lady," Jen said somberly.

"Right," Zeke agreed. "We know it must have something to do with a guest at the B&B because we saw the driver talking to someone."

"It had to be either Pierre or Mr. Richards," Jen reasoned. "The rest of the guests are part of a bird-watching organization. I'm sure they wouldn't want a tiger."

"But why would Pierre want to steal his own tiger?"

"What would Mr. Richards do with one?"

Their food arrived at that moment, and for a

while they were too busy eating to talk. When they finished, they decided it was still too early to go to the circus, so they headed down to the Mystic Marina. Zeke loved sailing and he enjoyed inspecting the yachts and sailboats tied up at the docks.

Some time later, Jen was surprised when she looked at her watch to find it was already ten o'clock. She called to Zeke, who was talking to the skipper of a 60-foot sailboat called the *Rakassa*.

Zeke waved to show he'd heard her, and a few minutes later he trotted over to where she was sitting on a piling, waiting for him. "Joe said he'd give me a tour of the *Rakassa* later," he said, beaming.

Jen rolled her eyes. She didn't like sailing—it made her seasick. "What about the case?" she asked. "We only have until five-thirty to solve it. You don't have time for a tour."

Zeke knew his sister was right. The most important thing right now was to find Lady and figure out who had stolen her. He took one last wistful look back at the beautiful sailing yacht. He wished he could spend all day sailing.

"Come on," Jen said, pulling him away.

They rode up Main Street, took a left on Fuller Road and then a right on School Street. The colorful circus was already noisy with music and it looked like all the rides were running. Winding between the crowds, Jen and Zeke kept their eyes open for anything that looked suspicious.

"Hi," said a boy about their age. He wore a red-and-white T-shirt and red shorts, and his brown hair was slicked back as though it were still wet.

"Hi," the twins responded, staring at him blankly.

The boy smiled at them. "What are you two up to?" He gestured with his right hand and in his left he balanced a coffee cake that was wrapped in a plastic bag.

Jen and Zeke glanced at each other. *Who was this kid? Did they know him from school?*

"Uh," Zeke said, "we're just, you know, checking out the rides."

"You have to try the Whoozy Doozy," the boy urged. Again he waved his right hand.

Suddenly, Jen laughed. "Mitchell!" she exclaimed.

The boy's eyes widened. "Huh?"

Now Zeke caught on, too. "Mitchell, we didn't recognize you at first," he admitted. "You look totally different without your clown makeup on."

Mitchell grinned. "You mean you didn't even know it was me?"

Jen shook her head. "Not until I recognized the way you wave your hands around when you talk.

We've never seen you without your wig and costume and makeup on."

Mitchell laughed. "I forgot about that. Hey, I'm taking this coffee cake over to Mr. Zambini's trailer. My mom made it because she feels bad about his accident. Mrs. Zambini said he's in their trailer, resting. Want to come along?"

Zeke shrugged. "Sure."

They followed Mitchell behind a roped-off area that had a sign reading RESTRICTED—CIRCUS PERSONNEL ONLY. Mitchell led them to a cluster of trailers. "This is where we live," Mitchell explained. "Pierre's trailer is over there, but I guess you know that." He waved in another direction. "I live down that way, and here's the Zambinis' trailer."

It wasn't hard to miss. It was painted a dark purple and gold letters spelled out ZAMBINI across the side. Mitchell knocked on the door. No one answered.

"Maybe he fell asleep," Jen suggested.

"Maybe," Mitchell agreed. He tried the door handle. It turned. "Let's just leave this inside on the kitchen table. We don't have to wake him up."

They entered the trailer, tiptoeing and not speaking. Jen was amazed to see how much could fit into such a small space. There was a kitchen with a sink, refrigerator, stove, and oven, an eating area, and a living room with plush green carpeting on the floor. The bathroom door stood open, and two other doors farther down were open, too.

"The bedrooms are down there," Mitchell mouthed and pointed as he put the cake on the table.

Jen turned around and glanced down at the counter, which was covered with piles of opened letters. She noticed that the envelopes were holding what looked like bills. One pink sheet stuck out of an envelope and Jen could read the words "Final notice" written across the top in bold letters. Feeling guilty for spying, she moved toward the door.

Zeke stepped after her, then noticed the vase of flowers on the side table with a "Get well soon" card attached. One of the flowers in the arrangement was a lily. He tried to step away from the flowers as quickly as possible, but it was too late. His nose itched. Lilies always made him sneeze. He tried to squeeze his nostrils closed to stop the tickle, but it didn't work. A squeaky sneeze erupted. The three of them stared at one another, expecting Mr. Zambini to come groggily out of his bedroom at any second. But nothing happened.

"Either he's a deep sleeper," Zeke said with a sniffle, "or he's not here."

"Either way, we'd better get out of here," Jen said.

She led the way out of the trailer.

"I've got a while before I have to get into costume," Mitchell said. "Let's go on the Whoozy Doozy, my treat."

"Sure," Zeke said. One ride wouldn't hurt, but

then they had to get down to some serious sleuthing. Five-thirty would be here before they knew it.

Jen made a face. If sailboats made her feel ill, she could just imagine what the Whoozy Doozy would do.

The Whoozy Doozy line was long. The young man with the droopy blond mustache who was running the ride said that the regular ride operator was sick this morning and it had taken a while to find a replacement. He let Mitchell cut to the front of the line and they all got to ride for free. They strapped themselves into a small compartment just in time for the ride to start. The ride whirled slowly at first. Jen grinned. This wasn't so bad after all. But then the ride twirled faster and faster. Not only was the compartment going in circles, but the whole ride was turning as well. Jen began to feel green. She could see that Zeke and Mitchell were having the time of their lives, though. The ride continued spinning faster and faster. Jen closed her eyes, praying the ride would end soon. But it didn't. If anything, it seemed to turn even faster. And now it was bumping up and down, too.

She forced her eyes open and fear shot through her—not because Zeke was turning green, too, but because of the terrified look on Mitchell's face.

Something was definitely wrong!

"The ride is out of control!" Mitchell shouted.

10

The Million Dollar Question

Jen knew she'd pass out if the ride didn't slow down. Along with the whirling and bumping, there was now a loud banging sound. *What if the operator couldn't ever stop the ride? They'd be twirling around forever!*

Even as these thoughts careened through her head, the noise and bumping abruptly stopped. Slowly, the spinning decreased, but it seemed like it took forever. As soon as the ride stopped, Mitchell released the strap that held them in place.

"I wonder what happened," he said, shaking his head to clear the dizziness.

Jen scrambled off the ride. Her legs wobbled and for a second she thought she'd fall flat on her face.

Zeke grabbed her arm to keep her on her feet. They passed the ride operator, who was inspecting the gears of the ride with two men in gray jumpsuits. "Those are the circus mechanics," Mitchell told them as they walked by.

One of the mechanics scratched his head and said, "Looks like someone purposely jammed this gear."

Jen pulled Zeke aside. "Did you hear that?"

Zeke nodded. "Another act of sabotage."

Mitchell said he had to go put his clown makeup on and waved good-bye. As he trotted off, Jen and Zeke continued their conversation.

"But why would someone want to sabotage a ride?" Jen mused.

"So far there has been the Zambini accident," Zeke began, lifting one finger. He lifted another one. "And painting Pierre's trailer."

"Stealing Lady," Jen added. "And don't forget the clown noses and the stake in the ostrich cage."

"And now this ride." Zeke shook his head. "It doesn't seem to add up. Let's go home. I have a theory and there's something I want to look up on the Internet."

As soon as they got back to the B&B, the twins searched for Aunt Bee to tell her they were home.

As they neared the parlor, Zeke put his finger to

his lips. Jen heard someone talking—she recognized Mr. Richards's voice. The twins tiptoed so they wouldn't disturb him. Aunt Bee always reminded them that it was crucial to let the guests feel as if they were in their own homes and could talk on the phone without being disturbed, or even take a nap in the parlor if they wanted to.

Mr. Richards looked up at them and grinned. "Late this afternoon," he said into the receiver. "Don't worry." With that, he hung up, his diamond pinky ring flashing brilliantly. "What are you kids up to?"

Zeke shrugged. "Just looking for our aunt."

"Slinky, cut that out," Jen said as her Maine coon cat purred and rubbed against Mr. Richards's dark blue suit. She didn't normally warm up to the guests so quickly.

Mr. Richards laughed. "It's quite all right. I love cats and I miss all of mine." He rubbed Slinky's head and the cat purred even louder.

The three of them laughed.

"I think your aunt said she was going for a walk," Mr. Richards said.

Jen knew her aunt loved to walk along the bluff with the salty ocean breeze blowing her long gray hair. She could be gone for an hour or more. The twins excused themselves and hustled upstairs to

Zeke's room. He booted up his computer and signed onto the Web.

"What are you looking for?" Jen asked, flopping on a chair she had pulled up next to Zeke's. Her legs still felt a little wobbly from the ride.

"I memorized the license plate number on the truck. I just want to see if I can trace it."

Jen could hardly keep up with Zeke's fingers flashing over the keyboard and the way he flicked his mouse around. After ten minutes of investigating, Zeke sat back with a grin. "Check out this new Web site. It searches license plates for free, and it only takes seconds. . . ."

Jen leaned forward, anticipation tingling her fingers and toes. "So? Who does the truck belong to?"

Zeke put up his hand. "Just a sec. The computer is still searching."

They stared at the screen. Finally, a new image appeared. It listed the license plate number, the state in which it was registered, and the owner's name.

"The Pyramid Group?" Jen read out loud. "What's that?"

Zeke frowned. "It's the company that owns the truck. That must be why there's a black triangle painted on the side of it." His fingers flew over the keyboard again. He sat back in defeat. "The Pyramid Group must be the only company in the world that doesn't have a Web site. So we can't even find out anything about it or who the owners are."

Jen groaned. "A dead end."

"Hopefully not for Lady," Zeke said grimly, working at the keyboard again. "Let's look up the Big Top Insurance Company. I remember Pierre mentioning it."

They easily found the site and read the description of the company. "Insurance for all amusements, large and small. Put your trust in us. You lose, we pay!"

"It must be Pierre's insurance company," Jen said. "I wonder if he gets money for losing Lady?"

With Jen looking over his shoulder, he clicked on a policy information icon. They both read silently.

Then Zeke whistled. "The policy for rare animals covers up to a million dollars," he breathed.

Jen felt stunned. "That sure gives Pierre a motive for stealing Lady. It would take him months, if not years, of performing to make that much money from ticket sales. All he has to do is get rid of Lady and collect the insurance money and he's got it made."

Zeke thought for a moment and frowned. "But we still haven't figured out what all those other accidents and vandalism have to do with Lady's disappearance."

"Maybe he's trying to collect insurance on everything bad that happens?"

"That doesn't make sense. If he's trying to get the insurance company to pay for Lady, he wouldn't want to jeopardize that by having too many accidents happen or the insurance company might cancel the policy."

Jen nodded. Zeke had a point. "And it doesn't explain the clown footprint we found in the cage. When the tiger was stolen, Pierre was having a fit over his painted trailer."

They were both silent for a long moment, trying to sort out the clues.

"It'd be best if we could just find Lady," she said as she stood up. "Come on, we have to go look for her. If we find her we'll know who took her."

They hurried down the spiral staircase of the lighthouse tower, then stopped in the kitchen and grabbed sandwiches for lunch. Jen had one idea of where to look for Lady. She told Zeke about it once they were on their bikes and heading for town again.

"The old haunted house on Front Street would be the perfect place to hide a tiger," Jen insisted. "No one goes near that spooky place."

"But someone would hear if Lady roared."

"Well, it's worth a shot."

When they got to town, they headed for Front Street and rode south until they reached number 502, the old Murray mansion. They stood out front and stared up at the pointy roof peaks, the crumbling roof tiles, the broken and missing window shutters, and the peeling gray paint.

Jen shivered. Maybe this wasn't such a good idea after all.

Zeke took a deep breath. "Let's go," he said, sounding a lot braver than he felt.

They left their bikes on the pavement and passed through the creaking front gate. As soon as they walked onto the property, the sun went behind a cloud and everything became even gloomier. The front stairs groaned as they walked up them to the sagging front porch. A broken porch swing swayed in the breeze, one side of it still bolted to the ceiling of the porch.

"Think this is safe?" Zeke asked.

"No," Jen admitted. "But we have to find Lady before it's too late."

The front door was missing, so it was easy to enter the house. The high ceilings and dusty, dark drapes over the windows made Jen feel like she was entering a cave. It took a moment for their eyes to adjust.

Above them something creaked.

Zeke's heart slammed against his ribs. "What was that?" he hissed.

They heard another creak, followed by a loud thump.

Wide-eyed, Jen turned to Zeke. "It's either Lady or a ghost," she said with a gulp.

11

Haunted?

The twins cocked their heads, straining to hear.

"We have to go look," Jen whispered after a few seconds of absolute silence. She headed for the wide staircase that led up into the darkness of the second floor. They climbed slowly, watching and listening the whole way. On the second floor landing, they stopped and listened.

Zeke heard a shuffling sound down the hall to the left. He pointed. Jen nodded, and they headed in that direction. What if they came face-to-face with a hungry tiger? She gritted her teeth and kept moving. Now she could hear the noise again. It was getting louder.

Suddenly, Jen stepped on a loose floorboard. It screeched like a frightened cat, sending chills from Jen's toes to the top of her head.

"Nice going," Zeke whispered.

The shuffling sound stopped. Then they heard the sound of running feet. Jen and Zeke rushed down the hall. It zigzagged, then led to a second set of stairs heading down. Before they started down the stairs, they heard a bang below them.

Jen ran to one of the tall, dusty windows and peered out into the backyard. She gasped. "It's Mrs. Watson!"

The twins watched as their science teacher ran across the yard and scrambled through a gap in the back fence. Mrs. Watson took one last frightened look back at the mansion before disappearing from view.

"I wonder what she was doing here?" Jen said.

"She's been snooping around a lot," Zeke said. "She must be up to something."

They searched the rest of the house, but they didn't find Lady, or any ghosts, much to their relief.

Outside, it took a few minutes for their eyes to get used to the bright sunlight. When they could see again, they rode up and down every street, keeping their eyes open for any likely hiding place for Lady.

Jen gave a sigh of disgust as they reached Main Street. "Maybe we're completely wrong about what's going on. Maybe Lady really did escape on her own and the truck is for transporting goats or something."

Zeke gave his sister a look. "Are you kidding?

We've pieced the clues together perfectly so far. Everything makes sense."

They passed the Mystic Café on their left. Then they rode by the self-serve laundry and the Smith Sisters' Salon. Just after they crossed Front Street, Zeke whistled with appreciation. Mr. Richards's awesome roadster was parked in front of Perfect Pets. It gleamed in the bright sunlight. He had to stop and admire it close up.

"That is so great," Zeke said with longing.

"Yeah, and you only need, like, a million dollars to get your own," Jen said dryly. She looked around. "I wonder where he is?" Then she spotted him in Perfect Pets. "Let's see what he's buying."

They leaned their bikes against the wall, and stepped inside the store. Several people were in the store looking at the Persian kittens. One boy was begging his father for a pug. Mr. Richards stood near the counter with a large, bright blue-and-yellow bird on his arm.

"Nice parrot," Zeke said, walking up to him.

Mr. Richards turned and smiled at the twins. "It's a macaw. I've never seen one with such a beautiful blend of colors and such bright eyes."

As though the bird knew they were talking about him, he bobbed his head and squawked loudly.

Jen laughed. "He sure is a noisy guy."

"Oh, that's nothing," Mr. Richards said. "When you get thirty birds together in one aviary, now *that's* noisy!"

"Thirty of these guys?" Zeke asked.

Mr. Richards nodded. "I can't seem to stop buying them. My menagerie just keeps growing." He paid for the bird, then asked the twins if they needed a ride back to the B&B.

Zeke groaned. "I can't, I have my bike here."

"Maybe some other time, then. See you later," Mr. Richards said.

Jen and Zeke followed him out of the store and watched him pack the birdcage onto the passenger seat and zoom off.

Jen sighed. "We may as well head home, too. We haven't found out anything more and we're running out of time."

"We need to make suspect sheets," Zeke said. "It's the only way to sort everything and *everyone* out."

Back at the B&B, the twins settled themselves in Zeke's room. Jen grabbed a couple of pens and several sheets of paper and started writing.

Mystic Lighthouse

Suspect Sheet

Name: Pierre the Magnificent

Motive: Trying to make his show bigger and better; insurance money?

Clues: Why would he want to steal the star of the show? Is it worth it?

Was he the one talking to the truck driver?

The tiger was probably insured. Maybe Pierre would rather have the insurance money to upgrade the show?

What did he mean by telling Terra he was counting on her and why did that make her upset? Counting on her to steal the tiger?

Was the tiger stolen while he was distracting everyone with his ruined trailer? Is he working with someone?

Mystic Lighthouse

Suspect Sheet

Name: Mrs. Watson

Motive: Hates to see the tiger in captivity

Clues: Admitted she's against animals in captivity and says she'd do ANYTHING to let the tiger go free.

WHY WAS SHE SNEAKING AROUND THE SHOW AND NEAR THE TIGER CAGE? TO LET THE TIGER OUT?

WHAT WAS SHE DOING AT THE MURRAY MANSION?

Mystic Lighthouse

Suspect Sheet

Name: Terra the Tiger Trainer

Motive: Working with Pierre?

Clues: What was she talking to Pierre about after the trapeze accident? What did she mean by "You can trust me?" Trust her to steal the tiger? And what money was she talking about?

SHE WAS A CRYING WRECK AFTER TIGER DISAPPEARED—WAS SHE FAKING IT TO THROW OFF SUSPICION?

Was her key to Lady's cage really stolen or was she just trying to make it look like someone else could have done it?

Mystic Lighthouse

Suspect Sheet

Name: Mr. Richards

Motive: He collects exotic birds, could he collect other exotic animals, too?

Clues: WHY IS HE LURKING AROUND THE CIRCUS? WHAT CONNECTION DOES HE HAVE?

He admits he loves cats. Could he want a tiger? But he was on the phone all morning when the tiger was stolen.

Who is he talking to on the phone all the time?

HE TRAVELS ALL AROUND THE WORLD AND HAS BEEN TO SIBERIA. THE MISSING TIGER IS A SIBERIAN TIGER. ANY CONNECTION?

Mystic Lighthouse

Suspect Sheet

Name: ZAMBINI THE GREAT

Motive: MAD AT PIERRE FOR REPLACING THE GREAT ZAMBINI ACT WITH A TIGER?

Clues: Who cut their trapeze rope?

WHERE WAS MR. ZAMBINI WHEN HE WAS SUPPOSED TO BE IN HIS TRAILER RESTING?

Did he really hurt his leg, or was he faking it so he wouldn't have to perform? But why?

When the twins finished, they shuffled through the sheets again and again, but nothing seemed to sort itself out.

"Have we missed something?" Jen wondered out loud.

Zeke checked the clock on his desk. "I don't know, but we're running out of time!"

Note to Reader

Have you figured out who stole Lady? Is it the same person who is causing all the accidents at the circus?

If you review this case carefully, you'll discover important clues that Jen and Zeke have missed along the way.

Take your time. Carefully review your suspect sheets. When you think you have a solution, read the last chapter to find out if Jen and Zeke can put all the pieces together to solve *The Mystery of the Missing Tiger*.

Good luck!

Solution

Another Mystery Solved!

"It's five o'clock!" Zeke said. "The truck will be ready at five-thirty."

"Think!" Jen commanded.

"I *am* thinking," Zeke protested. He looked over the suspect sheets again. Something was niggling at the back of his mind. Something they hadn't written down on the suspect sheets. . . . Mr. Richards's ring!

"What?" Jen asked, sensing her brother's growing excitement.

"The Pyramid Group owns the truck, right?"

Jen nodded.

"Well, Mr. Richards wears a diamond pinky ring in the shape of a pyramid!"

Jen frowned. "That's not exactly solid evidence."

"Think about how he travels all over the world. He loves animals, right? He *collects* them."

Slowly, Jen nodded. "And he loved Slinky, even though she was leaving cat hairs all over his expensive clothes. And he sure is rich enough to buy a Siberian tiger."

"Exactly," Zeke agreed. "Tigers are so rare that if he couldn't find someone to sell him one, he'd have to steal it!"

Suddenly, Jen frowned. "But he couldn't have stolen Lady. He was on the phone all Friday morning, remember?"

For a moment, Zeke paused. Then he snapped his fingers. "He must have someone on the inside working for him. One of the clowns must be his partner. Which one? Who needs the money?"

Jen closed her eyes and thought about the clown clues. Which clown? Mitchell had said he didn't think any of the clowns would do it. And the shoes with the blue paint on them belonged to . . . no one.

"It's not a clown," Jen said finally.

"But what about the clown footprint?"

"It was an old costume. And remember how hard it was to recognize Mitchell without his makeup on? I only recognized him by the way he moved his arms around when he talked. Someone was wearing the clown suit as a disguise."

Something flashed in Zeke's head. "I saw a

clown," he said slowly, "on the morning Lady was stolen. I thought it was weird that he was in his costume already since none of the others were. He walked with a limp."

"*What* did you say?" Jen demanded.

"I saw a clown—"

"Did you say he limped?"

"Uh, yeah."

"Who is the only performer in the circus with a limp?"

Then it dawned on Zeke. "Mr. Zambini!"

Nervously he checked the clock again—5:07.

Jen also looked at the clock, then she jumped up and headed for the door.

"Where are you going?" Zeke called.

She motioned for him to follow her. As they raced down the stairs, she hurriedly told Zeke her plan between breaths. "The truck. We have to sneak into the back. It'll go pick up Lady. We'll find Lady. It's the only way—we'll get to her—before they get her out of town."

Zeke grabbed Jen's arm and hauled her to a stop. "Are you nuts?" he demanded.

"Do you have a better idea?" Jen asked, moving on again.

Zeke fumed. No, he didn't have a better idea, but

he didn't exactly want to be eaten by a tiger, either. On the spur of the moment, he stopped at the bee-hive-shaped kitchen phone.

"What are you doing?" Jen asked. "We don't have time for phone calls."

Zeke motioned for his sister to hang on for one second as he dialed Tommy's number. Busy. He tried again. Still busy. He tried Stacey's number and she picked up on the second ring.

Tripping over his words, Zeke tried to explain what was going on. "You need to find Pierre and call the police. Then get them to follow the truck that's at Tommy's uncle's garage. The one with the black triangle on the side. Tell Pierre it will lead everyone to the missing tiger!"

Stacey started to ask questions, but Zeke knew she could talk forever if he let her. "Just get going," he interrupted. "It could be a matter of life or death." *Ours*, he thought as he slammed the phone down and dashed after Jen.

With her wavy brown hair flying out behind her, Jen zoomed down the hill and headed for the garage, pedaling like crazy. They hoped the truck wouldn't have been picked up already.

As they rounded the corner, Jen sighed with relief. The truck was still there! The twins ditched their bikes and ran toward the truck, hunching down in hopes that no one would notice them. Zeke couldn't breathe until they had managed to lift the back door a crack and slip into the dark truck. When they slid the door back down, they were left in complete blackness.

Zeke breathed with relief.

"I hope the driver won't check back here before he takes off," Jen said, positioning herself against the wall so she wouldn't roll around when the truck started moving.

Zeke groaned. "Great. I never thought of that. And what are we going to do when they open the door to let Lady in? They're not going to be too thrilled to see us here."

"Don't worry. Stacey will call the police."

At that moment, the truck rumbled to life. Jen braced herself as the driver backed up and took a left out of the driveway. She tried to imagine where they were heading, but after several rights and lefts, she got lost.

Suddenly, the truck lurched to the right and Jen hit her head against the side as they bumped over a rough road before coming to a jerky stop. The motor cut off.

Jen froze. All of a sudden this did not seem like a great plan. She heard voices outside. Someone grabbed the handle of the back door and lifted. With a loud rattle, it flew up. Jen and Zeke stared right into the eyes of Mr. Richards and Mr. Zambini.

Zeke looked beyond the two angry men, but no police were in sight. They were doomed!

Jen recognized where they were right away. *Of course!* she thought. *The old, abandoned ballfield.* A dreadful thought was sinking in. What if the police hadn't followed the truck? Would anyone think to look for them here?

"What are you two doing in there?" Mr. Richards demanded.

"I—we—" Zeke began.

"We know everything," Jen blurted out, raising her voice to compete with the crashing waves nearby. "And you're not going to get away with it."

A slow smile spread across Mr. Richards's face. He smoothed one hand over his oiled hair. "Of course I am. I always do. How do you think I have collected so many exotic creatures for my menagerie?"

Mr. Zambini stood nervously at his side.

Then Mr. Richards's smile turned nasty. "Go get Lady," he ordered.

Mr. Zambini blanched. "What about the kids?"

"Exactly," Mr. Richards said. "We'll find out if Lady has any wild instincts left in her."

Jen gasped.

"You're going to be in big trouble for this," Zeke said boldly.

Jen looked at her twin in amazement. He sounded so sure of himself. Then the faint sound that Zeke had obviously already heard reached her ears. Sirens!

Very soon, Mr. Richards and Mr. Zambini also heard the sirens, but it was too late for them to escape. Two police cars zoomed down the dirt road and slammed to a stop, surrounding them. Right behind them a circus van kicked up dust as it stopped and Pierre, Stacey, Mrs. Watson, and Terra jumped out. The police immediately put handcuffs on Mr. Richards, Mr. Zambini, and the truck driver.

"You have a lot of explaining to do," one of the police officers growled.

"We can explain most of it," Jen offered. She told everyone how they had figured out all the clues and discovered who was behind Lady's cat-nabbing. She looked around. "But we didn't figure out that this old abandoned sports field would be such a great hiding place. It makes sense. No one comes here now that there's a brand-new field, so no one would see Lady, and the Atlantic covers up most sounds."

Zeke turned to Terra, who now had possession of Lady's leash. The immense tiger lay down patiently at her feet. "We thought you might be guilty," he admitted.

Terra's green eyes opened wide. "Me? Why?"

"We heard you arguing with Pierre, promising him money."

Terra smiled. "I was promising to make him money with Lady." She bent down and scratched the tiger's ears. "We make quite a team."

"The circus wasn't doing well," Pierre said. "I needed a new act to revive ticket sales. I was nervous that Terra's act wouldn't do it," he said sheepishly. "I'm afraid I was rather on edge and not very kind."

Jen faced Mr. Zambini. "You were the one who stole Terra's keys for the cage, right?"

Mr. Zambini nodded, not lifting his face to look at anyone.

"You were that jealous of the new act that you wanted to get rid of it?" Zeke asked.

"No, no," Mr. Zambini protested in his slight accent. "I needed the money for my son. He is in medical school and the cost is very high. He wanted to be a veterinarian. It was his dream and I wished it to come true. But I couldn't afford it. When someone told me Mr. Richards would pay one hundred thousand dollars for the tiger, I made my plans."

"You cut your own rope," Jen guessed out loud.

"And caused all the little problems like missing clown costumes and painting Pierre's trailer blue."

"Yes," Mr. Zambini admitted. "I thought if there were many things going wrong, and one of them happened to me, no one could suspect me. They would just think someone was trying to ruin the circus."

Jen and Zeke glanced at each other. "It worked," Jen admitted. "It wasn't until Zeke remembered seeing a clown who walked with a limp that we figured out it was you."

Zeke turned to Mr. Richards. "And we thought you were a banker."

"Why a banker?" Mr. Richards asked.

"We heard you talking about bucks," Jen said. "You said the more bucks the better."

Mr. Richards frowned. "I was talking about male rabbits."

Jen shook her head. "Rabbits?"

"A buck is a male rabbit. My supplier found several bucks with extremely unusual markings. I wanted them for my collection."

"What do you do with all your animals anyway?" Stacey asked. Jen noticed that her best friend had her pen and pad of paper out.

Mr. Richards shrugged. "Not much. I just collect them."

"Like a zoo?" Stacey persisted.

"A *private* zoo," Mr. Richards said. "I don't like anyone else looking at my animals."

"I think we've heard enough," the police officer said. He pulled on Mr. Richards's arm. "You three are under arrest. You're coming with us."

After they left, Jen looked at her science teacher. "What are you doing here?"

Mrs. Watson looked embarrassed. "I was at the circus to see if Lady had been found when the call came. I just jumped in the van before anyone could say anything, and here I am. I had to be sure Lady was safe."

"But why were you at the old Murray mansion?" Zeke asked. "We saw you there."

"That was you?" Mrs. Watson exclaimed. She laughed. "You scared the daylights out of me. Like you, I was searching for the tiger. I was afraid she was being abused."

Terra clucked her tongue. "I've examined Lady, and she's in perfect health. The robbers didn't hurt her, thank goodness."

Lady rubbed her massive head against Terra's legs. "Yes, I missed you too," Terra said with a laugh.

Mrs. Watson sighed. "It seems that Lady really likes you."

"Of course," Terra said. "I raised her from a cub,

saving her from terrible people who were trying to illegally raise white tigers for their pelts."

"How horrible," Mrs. Watson said. "I guess she really is better off with you. I'm sorry I made such a fuss."

Terra waved away her apology. "I understand. And believe me, I treat Lady like a *queen.*"

Stacey moved closer to the tiger trainer. "Can you tell me where you were born?"

Terra looked confused. "What does that have to do with anything?"

"It's background for the article I'm writing," Stacey explained, holding her pen poised above the paper.

"Always looking for a front page story," Jen said with a chuckle.

"Let's go to the circus," Zeke said. "With everything going on, we haven't had a chance to really enjoy it."

"We can look for Tommy," Jen said.

Stacey grinned. "Not that we'll have to look very hard."

"He'll be at the food stand," Jen and Zeke chimed in together. Then they burst out laughing.

About the Author

Laura E. Williams has written more than twenty-five books for children, her most recent being the books in the Mystic Lighthouse Mysteries series, *ABC Kids*, and *The Executioner's Daughter*. In her spare time she works on the rubber art stamp company that she started in her garage.

Ms. Williams loves lighthouses. Someday she hopes to visit a lighthouse bed-and-breakfast just like the one in Mystic, Maine.

Mystic Lighthouse

Suspect Sheet

Name:

Motive:

Clues:

Mystic Lighthouse

Suspect Sheet

Name:

Motive:

Clues:

Mystic Lighthouse

Suspect Sheet

Name:

Motive:

Clues: